BAKER STREET

UNIVERSE TALES 6

John Pirillo

NIGHT WITCH

In the darkness

In the darkness it follows,

Its eyes demon bright

A heart not deep, but shallow

Its soul has lost its light.

It lives in the past

Soul all aghast

Troubled and plighted

By the life now past.

Searching for nothing

But to bring sorrow and pain,

It wallows in self pity

Its life dark and restrained.

-- Doctor John Watson

it follows

Baker Street nestles snugly in radiant pools of light and intermittent pools of shadow along its length. The Tesla powered streetlights along its sidewalks dimmed this time of night. Set to lower their intensity once MidBells struck. No Londoner of a sound mind dared to walk the streets alone and unprotected these days once the night had a firm grip on the day once more.

Yet, there are always a few...foolish or brave.... or just with no other choice...who dare the night and its shadowy denizens.

Sheldoon McConnery is one of them. Sheldoon is a tall man, a bit stooped from the hard labor he does, his brown hair starting to turn white at the ears, and brown eyes filled with a light that can only shine when someone knows what they are leaving is only going to be better when they return.

He opens the door to his flat, turns about and gives his dear wife, Gaea, a hug, and kiss. "I promise, I won't forget the bread this time."

She laughed and pinched his cheek. "It's not the bread I'm aworried about, dear Sheldoon."

He feels a rush of pleasure in his lower parts. She did not have to spell it out. She knew and he knew exactly what she was referring to. As do all newlyweds, unable to part without a pinch in their hearts, and perhaps other spots of their bodies as well.

"Glad of that I am, Ms. Tilde McConnery, the blossom of my life, the honey of my heart."

She laughed. "Flattery will get you everywhere!"

He smiled. "I'm counting on it!"

"Go, before you cause my clothing to size with fire from your burning love."

He laughs. "Well, that may be so, but later there will be bread. That I promise. I will not forget. I swear upon my life and soul," he promised, crossing his heart.

She laughs again and kisses him more deeply on his mouth. Pulls back. Grins like a hungry wolf. Just do not forget I have butter for your bread you promise me."

He laughs. "Now that would be downright folly for me now, wouldn't it?"

She swats his behind. "Now get ye to work, so your bread will be back in time for breakfast."

"And don't forget the butter," he adds teasingly.

She smiles. "You would never let that happen!"

"So right you are, my honeybee!"

He laughs and steps down to the sidewalk. Turns. "Tilde, dear Tilde, surely you own me heart and me soul as surely as the moon owns the Earth."

She burst into laughter. "Foolish Sheldoon, everyone knows that the Earth revolves around the moon, but only because he is so handsome."

Sheldoon barks with laughter. "Surely, that is God's truth, it is!"

He gives Tilde a wink and begins walking as fast as he can for the nearest bus stop. The bus will not wait for him if he is late.

A big mistake.

Because now he will be into much of a rush to be as cautious as he should be, he thinks as he scurries along at his best pace.

As he hurries along, more mindful of where he has been, than where he is now, a shadow shifts from a pool of darkness behind him swiftly into another. Working its way closer and closer to him.

Sheldoon stops once and looks about, shivers, but sees nothing. Goosebumps pop on his arms and neck.

"Worry not, Sheldoon. Shadows cannot hurt a fly!" He tries to reassure himself.

He swallows his fear and begins hurrying once more, but this time not because he might miss the bus, but because he might not make it that far.

No one, this late at night, in their right mind genuinely believes it's absolutely safe to trave this late at night...even though the famous Sherlock Holmes lives on the same street.

Holmes is not a god, merely a mortal like Sheldoon, and right now this mortal had better move faster yet if he wants to make it to work.

Behind Sheldoon, scooting from one pool of darkness to the next, paralleling Sheldon's path, the shadow flees what little light there is to reach the next pool of darkness.

Each time it moves, it is closer yet to Sheldoon. Only a few yards of sidewalk between them.

Sheldoon does not realize that when he crosses the street to get into a bit more of light to see his way by, that this was the intent of the shadow following him. Sheldoon is now urged along through his fear, the growing number of goosebumps on his neck and arms, the cold sweat on the back of his neck. Pushed by his urgency and building desperation to get away from something he feels but cannot see. Getting closer and closer to where the shadow wants him to be.

The shadow can almost taste the final moment in its dark soul as Sheldoon nears where he would not go if he knew better. But Sheldoon does not know!

Sheldoon has not an inkling that his destiny is not with bread or work this day, but a far less pleasant, and far more unpleasant and painful cessation of what he lives for. He still believes he is safer and safe if he keeps moving, does not stop.

And that is what fear can make you think, even when it is far from the truth!

"Hate this!" Sheldoon swears as he pushes himself harder, almost running now.

His fear is now dragging the past before his mind, and that does not help one bit. Not one! Sheldoon muses as he hurries along. His breath like fire in his chest, eyes tearing up, skin growing cold and clammy with sweat. Hair raising on his scalp.

Isle of Scots

Sheldoon is a Scotlander by birth, from the Isle of Scots. A part of England that broke off during the Skeleton Wars, its population shattered by the massive earthquakes and tsunamis that struck the remaining portions of the land.

But not all perished. The survivors soon repopulated the new isles, putting up flags on trees and any high spot to let the world know they were alive and were not giving up. To show their determination to survive and to bring in women and men to rebuild their population. During the early days of their new growth, all immigrants were welcome, and not much attention paid to the quality of those who wished to settle down.

But there came a day when Scotlanders would pay a price for their rush to become secure and great once more. A terrible price.

Not even the Great Resurrected King, Loch of Lochmar, was able to stop the sudden wave of evil that swept across the isles. Evil which had hidden among the new settlers, seeking a new birthing place, and food!

But there came a day when the Night Witches were held accountable. By the help of the English. It was a terrible war. When it finally abated, too many brave men and women had died. But just like when Scotland was broken, the tide of evil was destroyed once mor, driven off the Isle of Scots.

There are scholars and historians who say it was Merlin, the Great Magician, who stepped in on behalf of humanity. Not the might of the English Army. They claimed it was merely that evil knew its numbers were too weak to sustain a constant clash with the Scotlanders.

Others, who were wiser, and more knowledgeable, knew the fading of evil was something much more than the sum of the two. That a shift in power was about to happen. Evil was not withdrawing but hiding once more. Until it could rise once more. More powerful. And unstoppable. They just did not know when or how that would happen.

But, to the delight of the Scotlanders, while it the pause of the war gave them a chance to breathe again and regather their strength; the affliction of the Dark Angels, as the terrible ones were now called, had not been chased from the Scots, but instead had migrated to

England, there to become a blight upon the goodness of its people.

So, the remaining Scotlanders counted their blessings, sought blessings wherever possible, and prayed they would be strong enough to endure the coming years. Be prepared for a battle they also prayed would never happen, but more than likely would come, like it or not.

The only problem was that while the Scotlanders had an inkling of the coming darkness. The poor English, arrogant with newfound wealth and power from their battle with the Dark Isles, had no idea what had infiltrated them. Brought back unknowingly by the weary veterans of the war in the Scots

And now the Night Witches were regaining their numbers.

Their strength.

Hidden.

Watching.

Waiting for the right moment.

Sheldoon, this time, not only saw the shadow scoot across the street to follow him, but he also heard a nightmarish cry. Low and filled with a vibration that rattled his brain and shook his sense.

He now realized he was at the center of a conflict that he thought was of legendary history, not the immediate present. And he would be at the forefront of the coming battle.

Battle for survival.

For power.

For control.

And the unthinkable!

So, now It followed.

He moved a step.

It moved a step.

He turned to look, and it flit back into the shadows nearest him. Carefully, cautiously, not because of it being uncertain or fearful of the outcome of a confrontation. Far from it.

It follows.

Its nature.

It is way of life.

It follows.

And then…

The Shadow no longer hid but lashed out with power so terrible that Sheldoon gasped.

His heart suddenly stopped beating and he felt as if ice had suddenly clutched his entire body in an unbreakable grip.

He staggered, like a drunk man might, uncertain of his step and even where he was, or what he was stepping on or into.

He no longer felt fear and terror.

He was an animal crazed by it!

Constable Fry

Constable Fry, on his usual beat, making the rounds of Baker Street, was in a great mood.

Not a single drunk.

No Midnight Angels.

No hint of shapeshifters, or even of ghosts tainted this wonderful night for him.

Baker Street, extremely often, seemed to be the epicenter of the most dangerous and dark sort that walked this end of Baker Street.

He felt so elated, in fact, that he began whistling. Something he usually did when alone at home or with his mate at the local pub. But not on these beats. They were often too fraught with the unthinkable, theft, the dead and the dying.

His mates got the better, richer areas of town. The only squeaks of violence there were the clinks of champagne glasses and the titter of slightly inebriated Night Angels, going along with the inebriated, pretending they were seduced, and later taking their money.

Sherlock Holmes lived on the other end and this street had to be one of the safest in all of London, fiends and villains knowing that he would not tolerate their presence. But more importantly, that he had friends who were quite familiar with fighting crime and the supernatural. But tonight, for some reason, it all felt different for Constable Fry.

He started to whistle anyway, needing to cheer himself up now, instead of just passing time.

That is when he heard Sheldoon's scream.

Constable Fry, to his credit, did not flinch from his duty, but took his nightstick out. The one with the silver tip for the supernatural. He did not run into them all the time. But on the rare time he did, a bit of silver usually came in quite handy. Anything less would not stop them.

He burst into a run as a second cry filled the night. But this time it was not fear he heard, but the cry of a dying man in great pain!

Sherlock Holmes sits on his bed, a narrow mattress beneath him, with a simple wool blanket and white sheet about his legs. His back supported against several oversized pillows. His eyes shut, and his hands on his blanketed lap, one over the other.

One might think him dead were they unfamiliar with his skills and knowledge because he does not appear to be breathing. But in fact, Sherlock Holmes is deep in a meditation he learned in India.

A look of peace and contentment suffuse his expression. What mystics call a state of Samadhi. Where the ego no longer dominates. Only peace and harmony remain.

Unfortunately, for Holmes, his state of peace is at once dramatically broken by a distant scream through his open window.

Front Porch

Holmes finishes shrugging his cape and hat on, then hurries down the front porch to the sidewalk, where Constable Evans is already waiting for him.

"Where?" Holmes asks.

"This way. I was meeting up with Constable Fry to go the Black Dragoon at the wharf, when Inspector Bloodstone caught up with me."

Holmes smiled at the kindly faced young man. "You made the mistake of telling him where you were going."

"Obviously." Constable Evans smiles. "Hard not to, when you're both living in the same flat."

"Maybe it's time to live on your own, Constable Evans."

"What! And miss all the fun? Fat chance."

Constable Evans points the direction they must go. "Watson is already there."

"Ah, that explains why he never replied to my call."

"You two are an odd couple, aren't you?"

Holmes gave Constable Evans an easy smile. "Of that you can be sure. Come, the game is on, and we have work to do, have we not?"

They hurried down the street.

Behind them something moved in the shadows. In the deepest of them, watching. But not for long.

Soon after they left, it drifted, a shadow among shadows along the building walls across the street, paralleling their path.

It follows.

It is curious.

It must know.

So, it follows.

Constable Fry stands silently at the nearest streetlight, his weight against it, holding a wet cloth to his forehead.

"Better, Constable Fry?"

Constable Fry nods to Watson, who nods back in satisfaction, then returns his attention to the various canvas tarps that lay over body parts up and down the alley he stands in the throat of.

"Nasty bit of business," he signs.

Constable Fry does not reply to the statement. He is having hard enough time keeping his gorge down as it is without remarking further on the most disgusting murder scene he has ever investigated.

One day this alley could very well become as famous as that of White Chapel.

He at once wiped that horrid thought from his mind. His father had told him of that one, and he had no desire to be part of anything like that.

He prayed not, but one never knew. After all, supernatural crimes had pretty much the same outcome as a criminal one. Except, oftentimes, but not always, it ended up more tragically and for many, more gruesome deaths than just one man could account for.

As Watson gazed at the tarps, and the nervous constables who guarded them, he had no doubt this death was not normal in any sense of the word. There was no known weapon...to him at least...that could have caused this much carnage and drained all the victim's blood at the same time.

Not a drop of blood stained the pavement, or the body parts discovered. Watson took samples in various spots where blood might have been to examine later in the Cold Room. A deep and cold room in the Scotland Yard, where the bodies of recent victims are stored, and autopsies done for clues.

Later, Watson, once this night's work was over, would return to the Cold Room to study the remains and the samples. But he had little hope they would contain any useable clues.

He sighed. Shivered.

Jumped.

A cold hand had suddenly pressed his shoulder.

"Sorry, John."

Watson sighed with relief and turned to give Holmes a quick nod. "A bit of a bloody mess, this one."

He gave Holmes a quick once over. "No gloves? No wonder you startled me so."

"Sorry, Watson, but it seems I was in a bit of a rush."

Watson nodded, but still seemed tense. Holmes could see that as plain as a shadow in the bright sunlight.

"But that is not what made you jump, is it, Watson?"

Holmes went to the nearest tarp and shrugged it free revealing the horrified face of Sheldoon, tears frozen on his cheeks. "No amount of blood loss would leave a man with frozen tears on his cheeks. And there is no blood to begin with, is there?"

He looked to Watson. Watson nodded. "Not a single drop, though I sampled spots that were stains on the cobblestones."

"But not blood."

"If blood, then not of any human type."

Holmes nodded. Shrugged a second tarp free to reveal a shriveled hand, skin baggy and winkled, like a shrunken balloon might appear after it popped. "And apparently, whatever struck this poor man, overwhelmed him so quickly, he hadn't a chance of defending himself."

"Why do you say that?"

Holmes dropped to a knee, held up the hand. "See the nails of his right hand. Perfectly clean. I would bet you that the other of his left as well."

Watson tugged a third tarp free to reveal the mangled, shriveled form of the left hand. It looked exactly

the same as the right one did.

Watson knelt over the hand a moment and sighed. "Exactly the same."

Holmes nodded. "There is no need to examine the rest of this man's body."

"No there is not. Had he been able to resist, even a bit he would no doubt have had something beneath his nails. But all are perfectly clean."

"Constable Fry, did you find any form of weapon on this…uh…victim?"

Constable Fry tried to reply, but he could not hold the gorge down any longer. He rushed out of the alley to throw up.

Watson shook his head. "Death is not a pretty thing, I'm afraid," he commented at the sound of Constable Fry throwing up.

Holmes ignored the comment, looked at the two hands a long time, making mental notes of what he saw.

"Too clean!" Holmes said rather tersely. "Perfectly clean."

"How is that possible?" Inspector Bloodstone demanded, his loud voice pinpointing the direction from which he was approaching.

He ignored Constable Fry, no doubt as a kind gesture, but also because the man was obviously too distraught to give any feedback.

He made a note to himself to give the poor man a day or two of leave to recover. God knows he had needed it the first few times he had seen such ghastly deaths as this one appeared to be.

He looked back to his car, he had quicky parked at the entrance to the alley.

Its giant rooftop electric turbine was even now slowing down, the usual arcs of electricity about it, vanishing.

He sighed.

Just wished that this case could as easily vanish. But it would not.

He reached Holmes and Watson. "Tell me what you know."

He glanced at his son and rolled his eyes towards Constable Fry and his son, Constable Evans, his mop of red hair every bit as thick and lustrous as his father's, rushed off to console the poor man.

Pahalgam, India

Giant boulder overlooking the Ganges.

Night.

A much younger Sherlock Holmes sits on the edge of the giant boulder, soaking up the warmth from its huge body that the stone had absorbed over the day.

His eyes were closed, but he stirred slightly at the approach of the Monk, who had come forth as quietly as possible to join young Sherlock, his student.

"The night is so peaceful. Even the roar of the Ganges below seems respectful of it. And this boulder is better than my blanket where I sleep at night."

"It does and it is," the Monk replied as he sat next to Holmes. He patted Holmes on his right shoulder. "You are getting better, young Sherlock, in sensing my presence.

"Does this mean your hearing is better, or you are relying on more than your obvious senses."

Holmes smiled. "I've had a good teacher," Holmes replied, knowing full well the Monk knew exactly which it was.

The Monk folded his hand into his lap over his orange robe, his legs gathered beneath him in a traditional half yoga posture. He chuckled. "And what have I taught you that you could not have learned yourself eventually?"

Holmes laughed.

The Monk grinned at Holmes. The young man was brilliant, sensitive, and had a profound sense of humor. He would go far in this world."

His mind opened wide a moment, as if peeking into the future, and he thought, "He will need to go far!"

No other word passed between the two for a long time, until a huge owl flew over their heads. The bright light of the full moon amplified its shadow across them as it passed. The shadow gave the small bird the appearance of something quite a bit larger, as if a monster might be preparing to attack.

It called out in a screeching sound as it passed over them, to something, or somewhere only it could sense or see.

Both men thrilled to its call.

"The obvious is not always so obvious," the Monk finally spoke up after the owl had passed, now screaming as it passed over the mighty Ganges rushing below the foot of the boulder.

"Meaning?" Holmes inquired, knowing the Monk was in a teaching mood, and if so, he needed to stay sharp.

"That in the future you will face the obvious, which is also seemingly impossible. What do you do, then?"

Holmes picked up a pebble and tossed it at the waters below. It made no sound or splash, the waters of the powerful Ganges. Holmes had heard that the Ganges was a meeting place between heaven and Earth. Also, that it had created by the Indian goddess, Ganga, who sacrificed herself by lowering herself from heaven to purify and uplift the souls of 60,000 who had died horribly.

"Use logic."

"And?"

"Deconstruct the clues one by one."

"And then what?"

Holmes gave it further thought, then said. "Reach beyond the impossible for the possible."

"What would you find then?"

"The truth."

It Follows

It follows in the night,

The moon so bold and bright.

Like a soldier on duty,

Too long and tired,

Its eyes never see truly.

But drift like angry clouds,

Seeking that which we cannot know.

It follows because it must.

It must because that is its truth.

That is its nature...

Revenge and death.

--Doctor John Watson

Night Witch

Tilde McConnery sat alone and dismally upon a chair in the interrogation room at the Yard. The chair seemed much harder, and much colder than it should. She could barely restrain the pain in her heart, or the tears in her eyes.

It had been hard for Constable Evans to bear when he had waited with her for his father and the others, so he had excused himself on the pretext to fetch something warm and to eat.

Which he would have done anyway as the others were running late, but the way she kept looking at him mad him uncomfortable. He had a tender heart, his father told him, and it made him much too vulnerable to the feelings of others...especially women, of whom he had little experience as of yet.

Constable Evans brought in a tray piled with scones, biscuits, tea, and coffee and set it before Tilde. "Father...I mean Inspector Bloodstone wanted you to have some nourishment before we began."

She gave him a surprised look when he said father, but quickly recovered her composure, and attended to the food and drink he offered.

Constable Evans smiled. She seemed pleased at his offering. But then he would, being young and vulnerable to the wiles of a woman as of yet.

She wiped at her eyes, turned to pour herself some coffee. She needed to be awake, not fall back into the dreams she had the night before. She could not let those dreams hold her back from what must be done now.

She took a sip, and beamed at Constable Evans, fluttering her eyes warmly. "You're a kind man, Constable Evans."

He gave her a gentle smile and nod. "Thank you. But I want you to know I feel for your loss."

She blushed. "You're such a good man."

Then she set down her coffee hard, threw her hands over her face and burst into sobs.

Constable Evans did not wait. He sat next to her and pulled her gently to his shoulder. He could feel her pain. But he could also feel her warmth. Somehow, it felt comforting and disturbing at the same time. He began to feel guilty about it, but she sobbed against him, harder and harder. He did not have the heart to pull back or disengage from her.

He wanted to. His father would not be pleased were he to walk into the room now. And more than anything he did not want to anger his father or disappoint him.

But he also could not ignore the obvious pain of this distraught soul next to him. It hurt his heart so much to see the pain in her face and feel the loss in her sobbing.

So many times, now over his short career here at the Yard, he had comforted many another poor soul. It never got any easier. It never hurt his own soul less.

Little did he realize his father was proud of his son for this empathy, even if he sometimes chided Constable Evans, or otherwise reprimanded him.

"Ah-hem!"

Constable Evans gently disengaged Tilde from him. 'You ready for this?" He asked, giving Holmes a grateful smile for the warning.

Tilde nodded, but he could tell she was just braving it. Anguish in her eyes, lines of doubt, fear and distress in her face was excruciating to Constable Evans's good heart, and he was sure Holmes noticed it too. As he did not hurry anything up and actually stopped Constable Evan's father, Inspector Bloodstone, at the door long enough for Tilde to pull herself back together enough to go on.

Finally, she sat away from Constable Evans, and he rose and took his place by the door as Holmes, Inspector Bloodstone, and Watson Bloodstone entered.

Holmes sat opposite Tilde, and Watson at the far right and the Inspector next to Holmes.

Holmes was about to speak, when Tilde spat on the floor and gave him a look that was quite full of anger and hatred. "Night Witch!"

Holmes looked startled, as was Inspector Bloodstone, but Watson responded quite differently. He stiffened as of someone had just slapped him hard on his face and challenged his honor.

Holmes noticed. "Watson?"

Watson shook his head. "Not now. Later."

"Excuse me, Inspector," Watson said as he got back up and headed for the door. "I suddenly remember something I forgot to bring with me from the Cold Room."

Watson exited the room.

Inspector Bloodstone looked to Holmes. "Holmes? Have you any idea of why Watson just left our investigation?"

"None whatsoever, Inspector."

Holmes got up to follow Watson and left the room.

Inspector Bloodstone pushed his notepad in front of him, lifted a pencil and then eyed Tilde. Frustrated, but also realizing that Holmes and Watson had a special relationship, which he did not dare to deny them if he wanted their help. He sighed, also knowing that he must push on anyway. "Now, to begin with, Ms. McConnery. Could you tell us everything that happened that night before your husband, Sheldon...?"

"Sheldoon," she corrected him.

"Sheldon left for work?" Inspector Bloodstone asked.

He wrote Sheldon on his note paper. Tilda shook her head. "Not Sheldon, Sheldoon!"

"Ah! Pardon me," Inspector Bloodstone replied. He crossed out the name Sheldon he had on his paperwork and corrected it to Sheldoon. "Sheldoon, it is. Please, Ms. McConnery, let us go over everything you can remember from last night."

Tilde looked ready to cry again.

Gently this time. "Please, it's important to have every bit of information so we can bring your husband's killer to justice!"

She gave him a harsh look. Her face transformed with a monstrous rage disturbing her natural beauty, distorting it, and making her look appalling. "You'll never bring justice to me!"

Inspector Bloodstone paled, then quickly recovered. "Please!"

Tilde covered her face with her hands as if about to cry.

Inspector Bloodstone paused, saw the grief and pain
building in her face when she removed her hands. Quickly, he gave her a handkerchief. She blew her nose into it, then began to sob.

"I am sorry. Please forgive me. Let us continue."

"Thank you, Ms. McConnery. Please do," the Inspector urged her.

Tilde nodded, smiling faintly, she began, "It was our honeymoon night. And now I will never see him again. I will...."

She began sobbing loudly.

Inspector Bloodstone rolled his eyes in disgust and got up. He gave Constable Evans a nod. "Help her and let me know when she's ready to talk further."

Inspector Bloodstone got up and left the room to his son, Constable Evans, who at once sat next to Tilde and gave her his shoulder again.

This time she threw her arms around him and sobbed as if her heart were about to burst in her chest.

Constable Evans shut his eyes.

How can people be so cruel to each other? He thought. *"What kind of monster just ups and kills someone they don't even know like what happened to Mr. McConnery? What kind?"*

"John, I fear for our men," Captain Strickland admitted, as he cleaned his bayonet.

John Watson, a strapping young man, once eager to battle and protect his nation, found no pleasure in the words. The brief year of war, so far, had accelerated him into an adulthood he embraced weakly, but did not avoid. And what was worse, the food stank, was often rank with mud and dirt because of the trenches they slept in. And even worse yet, there were no scones.

Some things may change in a man's life, but for Watson, his mother's scones would always inhabit the better part of is heart.

He scrubbed his too long hair from his eyes and shook his head. Not in denial of what his captain had just said, but in agreement. Good reason to fear for their safety, the Night Witches…aptly named so, could take on the appearance of anyone.

Their biggest trick was to take on the form of a young child they had murdered, then use that form to throw off a soldier, then murder them. Once they had done so and consumed his essence, they could then assume his form and invade the trenches.

There were no safe places anymore.

Men's lives were at stake, and he could not be squeamish about doing his duty. A nation was at stake as well. His nation. And despite all the miserable circumstance and conditions of his deployment, he was honor bound to perform his duties, even if it meant his death.

The captain lapsed into silence, as did Watson, but his mind was racing. He could feel the presence of the Night Witches, their evil persona exuding such darkness that if felt like an onerous weight upon his shoulders and back. He felt even more miserable, knowing they could sweep into the trenches at any given moment and kill he and the captain, but did not, because they were cruel and preferred torturing their victims.

It was a new form of evil and horror to the Englanders. Being tortured mentally, instead of physically.

The Chinas had fallen to the Dark Ones, a race of beings, both terrible and strong. The first wave of Englanders who had attacked this Dark Isle, had perished to the man.

As had the second and the third waves.

Now, the soldiers of the King, knew better.

Were better prepared for what they would face. Though little safer, growled Watson inwardly. Safety is always an illusion on any battlefield, but this one even more so.

He felt a great sadness for a moment.

The innocent they had thought were the civilians of the Isle…were not innocent.

They had the face of angels, but the strength, cunning, and evil of demons from the lowest of hells.

Not all the people, of course, but enough, so that they blended well, and were hard to spot, until it was too late. That is, until England f ought back with its own source of power: Merlin.

Merlin had risen from the vast abyss he had hid himself in beneath London, where he had set up a school to train future wizards. He had come forth to train men and women of the troops to be able to spot the evil ones.

That had been the beginning of true victory for England. Now, even if not as powerful as the Dark Islanders, they at least had a fighting chance.

Watson, and his good Captain Strickland, were at the front of the new lines of conflict, their battle wizards acting as spotters, so that the ground troops knew who was right and who was wrong to target.

Even so, the loss of good men was terrible.

The battle was turning, but at a great cost of men. A great cost to the civilians, who were human and used as lures by the Night Witches, to throw the English off.

Another terrible thing about the war.

Using civilians as targets to protect the Night Witches as they battled.

Watson kicked at the mud before him. Sighed deeply.

When the battle for dominance finally ended, the Dark Ones had scattered deep into the Chinas, and though still troublesome, were no longer the overpowering force they had once been.

221B Baker Street

"England declared victory," Watson sighed. "But they were wrong."

Holmes paced the sitting room like a tiger in a cage, hands clasped behind his back, pipe in his mouth…. but unlit, his eyes bright with energy.

He suddenly stopped and turned to look at Watson, who sat by the fire, a warm cup of tea in his hands, and a plate of scones untouched on a small stool next him.

"I did not know this, John."

Watson shrugged. "You can know a man all your life and still never plumb his depths entirely."

Holmes sat next Watson. "I believe those are words of wisdom purchased wisely in the marketplace of human values."

Watson smiled, finally took a scone, and nibbled a bite. Finished, he set it back down. "I think I will retire now.

He got up to leave.

Holmes rose suddenly and blocked his path. "But John, you have left out the most important part of your story."

Watson sighed. "I rather hoped you would miss that part."

Watson returned to his chair and sat back down, not eager for what he expected Holmes to ask of him. "But being who you are, and as long as I have known you, this comes as no great surprise."

Holmes sat down again too. "Taken the words right out of my mouth."

Holmes leaned forward expectantly. "Night Witch."

Watson took a deep breath.

"Tell me everything you know about them."

Watson shut his eyes.

What he told Holmes next dredged up memories that would trouble his sleep for many months to come.

A scream in the night

Watson sat polishing his bayonet while Captain Strickland fed a fire. Both were silent.

The night was extremely dark.

The moon gobbled up completely by a ravenous vacuum of space and stars.

Not even the whiff of a single cloud cottoned the skies that moment.

The serenity of the moment shattered by the ear-splitting scream of a man in great pain and terror.

Captain Strickland rose before Watson could and put a hand on Watson's shoulder. The captain armed himself with his service revolver. "Stay, john. I'll tend to this. Probably just Private Rogers having another nightmare."

"The gun?" Watson asked.

"A smart man can make dumb moves; but a smarter one anticipates those moves." He taps the muzzle of the pistol against the side of his skull. "Hence!'

Captain Strickland slips from the shelter of their tent into the night and vanishes.

Watson felt the blood drain from his face. He had just been told non-verbally that if the captain could not save Private Rogers, then he would make sure the Night Witches would not take him as well.

That image forced Watson from his momentary terror. Watson jumps up. 'To hell with this!"

He runs from the tent into the ghostly night, rifle in hand. Maybe it's time to do as suggested by Merlin and test the new metal of his bayonet...

Silver!

But it would only work if he were to strike the Night Witch in exactly the right spot.

And he would get only one chance to strike correctly.

If he missed?

That question haunted him as he ran to help his captain.

221B Baker Street

A loud pounding on the door startles Watson and Holmes.

Holmes nods his head. "Ah, Inspector Bloodstone."

He rushes from the room to open the front door below.

Inspector Bloodstone looks away from the street, his face rigid with fear, as Holmes opens the door.

"Inspector…"

"My son has vanished!"

Tilde's Home, the Sitting Room

Tilde sets a cup of steaming tea on her coffee table for Constable Evans, who nods with a smile, then pulls it to his lips to sip.

He sets it back down. "Ginger. My favorite tea."

She smiles. And sits opposite him, assuming an attentive pose.

He remains formal in his posture, even though he is seated. "I am here. You said it was urgent when you phoned earlier. And I am sorry, I could not come any sooner, we were still busy with…"

He lapsed into silence.

Tilde's eyes began to water.

But she restrained herself from crying.

A sound from the bedrooms beyond.

She glanced that way. "Oh dear! I'm afraid we've woke my little angel."

She gets up. "I'll be right back."

Constable Evans starts to get up. "I don't want to disturb your child."

"Oh, she's not my child," Tilde responds with a smile

and hurries into a bedroom, shutting the door behind her.

Constable Evans rises at once in alarm when the candles lighting the sitting room start going out, one by one, by one.

"Tilde!" He calls out, reaching for his night stick.

"What just happened?"

Inspector Bloodstone looks so miserable that even Watson feels sorry for the man he finds usually much too abrasive. Even the Inspector's usual full mop of red hair, which is usually neat and shiny, is hanging limp into his eyes, like a widow who has just lost her dearest.

Ms. Hudson enters the room and stops briefly at the appearance of the poor man, then she puts on a bright smile and approaches him. "Inspector, I hope you do not mind? I had some tea and coffee warming on the stove before you arrived."

She glanced at Watson. "I know John always feels better when he has his."

Watson rolled his eyes and she giggled, then set her tray down at the table next to the Inspector.

She picked up a porcelain cup with pink roses on its handle and set it down next the Inspector, then took the teapot up. The teapot was a burnished copper color with pink roses on its handle.

"Tea first, or coffee?" She asked cheerfully, the teapot wavering in her hand over the lovely cup before the Inspector.

Inspector Bloodstone eyes the scones near where Watson had been seated. "No thank you, but I wouldn't mind…"

Watson hurried to the stool and plucked the scones up. He gave the Inspector a strained smile. "I can spare one."

Ms. Hudson took the scones from Watson's hands and gave him a scolding look. She set them down before the Inspector and patted his shoulder, like she would a child. "There, there now, you just eat s many as you wish."

Watson rolled his eyes, but said nothing, as Ms. Hudson gave him a warning glance he could not ignore.

Inspector Bloodstone took a scone and gobbled it down so fast that he began choking on it. Watson was about to bawl him out for being such a slob, when the man broke into sobs. "Something bad has happened to my sweet young boy, I just know it!"

Holmes sat opposite the Inspector. "Tell us why you think that?"

Inspector Bloodstone nods, eats a second of the three scones on the plate Ms. Hudson sat before him, gobbles that down, again making choking sounds.

"For God's sake, man, stop keeping us in suspense," Watson growls.

Inspector Bloodstone grabs the last of the scones, gobbles it down, much to Watson's horror, then nods. "It's simple."

He looks into Holmes's face. "My son always returns home after work. Promptly. Never more than a few minutes earlier or later."

"And?" Holmes asks.

"He never returned home."

Inspector Bloodstone begins sobbing again.

Holmes glances at Watson, who looks ready to explode. He gives Watson a warning glance, then returns his attention to the distraught Inspector. "Tell me who Constable Evans last spoke with."

The Inspector shakes his head. "That woman whose husband died. She phoned him just before I left." He looks into Holmes's eyes. "Tilde. Tilde McConnery."

"How do you know that?" Watson demanded.

Inspector Bloodstone sat up straighter, blew his nose into a handkerchief, then said, "Because I related her message to my son. For some dratted reason, she seemed quite attached to the young man, what with his kind nature and all."

He shook his head angrily, making an even more disheveled mess of his red hair. He shook it out of his eyes and turned to Holmes. "I did not have the heart to deny a distressed woman the only source of comfort she seemed to accept."

Inspector Bloodstone wiped at his eyes that began moistening with tears again. "What harm could there be in that, I ask you?"

Watson gave Holmes an alarmed look.

"Watson?"

"There's something more about the Dark Ones that I haven't told you yet."

Watson made the mistake of not paying attention as he ran after Captain Strickland. He tripped on a boulder ahead of him and fell flat on his face.

The sound of a service revolver firing, then Captain Strickland's scream.

Watson jumped back to his feet and hurried ahead.

He reached the position where he had heard Captain Strickland scream.

Standing over Captain Strickland was a small child, with eyes as innocent looking as a baby's. It had Captain Strickland's right ear in its right hand and was nibbling on it, as one might a scone.

The child looked up at Watson, giving him a smile that shook him to the core.

Watson felt this dreadful pull on him at once. But before it could fully overcome him, he fired his rifle.

The child giggled. The bullet Watson fired hovered in the air before its face, held there by an invisible force.

The child turned its innocent looking face to stare into Watson's eyes, then it recoiled, glanced down, and saw the silver bayonet plunged into its chest. It turned into a swirl of dark smoke, which then blew apart as if a strong wind had blown across it.

Watson had taken the silver bayonet from his rifle, which he had fired with one hand, and jabbed the knife into the child's chest at the same time. The child's attention had been so locked on the rifle's barrel, that it had not realized the bayonet was missing until too late.

Luckily for him, he had been paying attention when Merlin said the Night Witches use their eyes to freeze you.

Watson at once dropped to Captain Strickland's side and felt for a pulse, but the man was dead, his flesh already as cold as if he had been dead for hours.

Watson looked into Holmes's eyes. "The Dark Ones cursed everyone who came to destroy them."

"And what does that have to do with this case, Watson?"

Watson's hands were shaking so bad he had to put his tea down before he spilled it. "Every man I served with during that war has died under mysterious circumstances."

Watson looked away. "Only one lived long enough to know what truly happened.'

He looked at Holmes again. "I."

"I am sorry, John. I had no idea."

"And let's pray you have no further experience with these creatures, for they can not be easily killed when they are transformed."

"How do you mean?"

"They take on the form of an innocent child only just before they tear you apart and then eat you!"

Holmes's eyebrows arched.

"Before that, they assume the shape of someone they had murdered before."

Tilde's Home, the Sitting Room

Constable Evans is heading for the door out when Tilde re-enters the sitting room. "Oh, dear, dear me. I have been such a rude host."

Constable Evans turns to look at her.

But she no longer looks like a grown woman. Now, instead of the long lustrous brown hair she had before, she has black hair, and her skin is black as coal, and she is a small child, but with a grown woman's voice.

She smiles. "Your father served in the China Wars."

"Who are you?" Constable Evans demands, reaching for his night stick.

He pulls it out, making sure the child sees the silver on its tip. "I'm well protected."

"If you say so," the child responds with a smile that turns Constable Evans's blood cold.

"Dark Ones?" Inspector Bloodstone asked, perking up. "Those savage witches from the Chinas? What do they have to do with this?"

Holmes cocked an eyebrow. "Inspector, did you fight in the China Wars?"

"Of course, I did. Every bloody man in my age group did. Well, except for the doctor here, just a young tadpole at the time."

He glanced at Holmes as if the man had gone stark raving mad. "What does that have to do with anything?"

Holmes went for his cape and hat. "I'll explain on the way."

"Way where?"

"Watson, make sure your service revolver is loaded with silver bullets."

"But they won't stop a Night Witch," Watson protested.

Inspector Bloodstone rose in alarm. "The blood of your children will be spilled..."

Watson finished for the Inspector, "...Even as you have spilled the blood of ours!"

"By God, Holmes, I did not put the two together until this moment."

Holmes smiled. "Hurry, we have a life to save!"

Holmes said no further and rushed down the stairs for the front door.

Tilde's Home, the Sitting Room

The child grinned at Constable Evans. "Because you were so sweet to me, I will not let you die without knowing the truth."

"I'm not ready to die," Constable Evans replied, hefting his night stick."

"All must die sooner or later," the child replied.

Again, Constable Evans felt as if his mobility was being sucked out of him.

The child approached slowly. "Your father fought in the China Wars."

"Yes. Yes. So?"

"A child for a child. So, it was said, and so it must be done!"

Constable Evans blanched with fear. "What do you mean?"

"All men who killed mine, must now die and their descendants." The child giggled, sending chills of horror through Constable Evans.

"Which means you...and later...your father!"

The child laughed, then began transforming into the most hideous being that Constable Evans had ever seen.

It rushed Constable Evans.

He threw his nightstick into its face, but it only bounced off.

The door to the room smashed open behind Constable Evans in an explosion of wood, lock, latch, and bolts, then Holmes, Inspector Bloodstone and Watson rushed inside.

"Now, Watson!"

Watson fired all six bullets in his service revolver. Silver bullets he had put into it on the way here.

The ghastly monster, with a hydra head of swirling semi-transparent snakes that had glowing red eyes, roared in anger, then in pain as first it was struck in its chest, then its neck, then between its three eyes.

It fell to the floor, only inches from Constable Evans.

It deflated like a balloon, its scaly skin and clawed feet and fingers shrinking until only the child shape was left on the floor before Constable Evans.

Holmes stood over the creature.

"May God have mercy on your soul."

"Son, are you all, right?"

A very shaken Constable Evans nodded to his father. "How is this possible?" He asked. "Tilde went in the bedroom and...and..."

Watson put a hand on Constable Evans's shoulder. "It's part of their dark magic."

Inspector Bloodstone put an arm about his son's shoulders and hugged him close. His eyes were wet with tears. "I thought I had lost you."

Constable Evans started to pull free, until he realized his father really meant it, and then tears rushed into his own eyes and he wrapped his arms about his father and returned the love he seldom got from the Inspector.

Holmes glanced at Watson.

Watson was shaking.

Holmes put a hand on Watson's shoulder. "Thank you!"

"For what?"

"Being the good man, you are."

Ms. Hudson latched the front door after Inspector Bloodstone and Constable Evans exited for their car out front. Both had a cloth sack filled with fresh raspberry scones she had made for them.

Constable Evans got in, looked back, and waved.

She waved in return and their car headed away.

She sighed.

Felt a warm hand clasp her side.

"John. However, in the world do you men manage to get into so much trouble all the time?"

Watson turned her about, his eyes twinkling. "It's part of our job."

She laughed, gave him a light kiss on the lips. "Tell me about it."

"I will. Later."

She smiled. Took his hand and led towards her flat. "I'm counting on it."

Watson muttered a silent prayer of thanks as she opened her door and led him inside.

A few minutes passed and Holmes came downstairs, cape and cap on.

He heard the sound of Ms. Hudson and Watson laughing from her flat. Paused a moment, smiled, then exited the building, whistling a new tune he had learned from Willie, William Shakespeare, at the Globe Theater several nights ago.

Harry Houdini stood waiting at the curb beside his electric car. "What about Watson?"

"Holmes has got a bit on his mind, this evening."

"I bet he does," roared Professor Challenger from the back seat of the car.

Conan, seated next to Challenger, grinned. "I just wish the two of them would hurry it up and get married. This is ruining all our fun."

Holmes climbed into the front seat besides Harry, who got into the driver's seat.

Harry laughed. "Conan, you should talk. You always have to pretend you're on a business call when we go out."

"I do not!" Conan protested.

"Go on telling yourself that," Harry shot back and gave the car full juice, sending them hurtling down the road before Conan could reply.

Sherlock Holmes

Cyclops

John Pirillo

Copyright 2021

Table of Contents

Grave of the Ancient One 4

Cyclops...9

Epitaph for A Friend................................13

A Lesson Well Learned Soon Forgotten.....................16

Londonderry Market..................................26

An Unexpected Turn of Events 30

Death's Call..32

221B Baker Street...................................35

The Second Crime Scene 38

Myth of Reality.....................................47

The Killer's Identity................................50

The Giant Stone 53

Happy Sunshine Flower Shop 58

Londonderry Market.................................64

Rooftop...65

The Black Goddess 66

Hold of The Black Goddess..........................70

Main Deck 79

The Hold 80

The Dock..83

Help Arrives Too Late.......................................84

221B Baker Street...87

Holmes' Room 92

Grave of the Ancient One

Mesmer grimaced unhappily as he pulled on a glove. The tombstone leaning awkwardly towards him was a dirty relic left behind from a darker past of humanity. It reeked of death. Of dying. Of pain and of agony.

His nostrils flared with the pungency of the odor, but he did not shirk what he must do. What he looked for drove him so powerfully, that not even the deepest and darkest pits of hell could dissuade him from his path.

Revenge!

The moment he touched the tombstone, a shriek tore the air about him and dark creatures of the night, hidden in the brush and overgrown weeds of this part of the cemetery burst forth in alarm.

Now, he was satisfied this was the one!

To be sure, he examined the bright stars above him. Dark fisted clouds were pounding their way across a hollow moon, which had been pale before, but now was darkening as the fists of rain and storm swept across its wan face and engulfed it.

This night, many in London would arise to the sound of massive, shattering torrents of rain and pounding, smashing lances of lightning and roaring thunder. But here, Mesmer stood in the center of the storm and was untouched. He smiled with pleasure at his power, then swept his gloved hand across the tombstone. Swiping years of unattended dust and grime from the name that a legendary hero had once carved in bright, gold letters upon the granite of the stone.

The grime caused the layers of accumulated dust to smear across the palm of his gloves, greasing it like coagulating blood. But that did not matter, his glove was already thick with the detritus of past jobs.

He sniffed the glove, then nodded to himself as if agreeing that he had come to a correct conclusion. Though what that conclusion might be would not be clear to anyone watching.

But one thing anyone could agree on, if they were watching, is that time is a far greater judge of what must happen than anything man or creature can guess at.

Dust from a thousand carriages, a thousand, thousand storms sweeping through the forgotten dead's homes paint the tombstones and now his glove. Painting the worn stones of the yard with leaves, torn, and worn by time, shriveled into wisps of what were once crisp, green proud products of oak trees. And clinging to them and about the leaves was dirt clogged with debris left by the casual tourists who came to get their kicks. Droppings of pigeons who perched for a time, or crows add to the grime and aging of the stones. As if the stones were a field to be plowed and made fertile by the splotches that the fowl spread so generously from above.

He lowered his glove, his poetic moment satisfied. He could not read the tombstone that well in the dark, but the scent of his glove confirmed all the better what his eyes could not be sure of.

Even so. He had to be certain, so he snapped his thumb and forefinger together, causing a flicker of light which fed upon itself and climbed higher and higher until his palm became like an open lantern. He held his magic light closer to the lettering.

"Ah!" The letters were well worn by the constant grinding of wind and dirt, rock, and dust, but seemed right enough to him. Still...

He leaned closer to read better. Frowned, then touched the worn letters with the fire of his magic. The magic slid from his palm and coursed about the lettering until the name of the dead, whose body lay beneath the sodden earth and grimy tombstone, was as plain as the moon in the sky overhead.

"It would seem Cyclops, that you have been alone and forgotten far too long."

He stepped back from the tombstone, bumping into an archangel statue on one side that was poised with a burning sword in its hand, facing a second one across from it.

His short size was overwhelmed by the shadow of the giant angel. More than likely bought by a rich landowner to mark his grave so he would be remembered. But now, lost to all memories, as all are in time.

He looked at them and grunted. Made a gesture with the hand of fire and both statues crumbled to dust and blew away as if a sudden gust had occurred.

It had not.

He returned his attention to the tombstone. He smiled. A twisted smile, filled with the laughter of an empty heart and a greedy mind.

"Come now, Cyclops, I have a little something for you to do before you can slumber further."

He blew softly on the fire in his hand, and it wafted into the air and then drifted to the lettering on the tombstone. The glowing lettering burst into fire, burning so brightly, the short man had to fend off the heat with his arms a moment, before able to come close again, to see the results of his work.

He drew further back as the light of the letters grew brighter still and then the tombstone began to rise slowly into the air, inch by inch, until it levitated above the ground, revealing a rough area of tossed weed, soil and discarded bones left by predators.

"Rise and greet your master, Cyclops!"

The short man laughed and raised his arms higher, the magic of darkness pouring from them like a waterfall of evil.

"Arise and meet your master!"

Cyclops

The forgotten gravesite began to stir like a thick soup, the leaves, grass, rocks, debris, bones and weed stirring about, churning, making soft chuffing sounds, then the voices of creatures not visible to the naked eye, eerie and terrible began to wail, murmur, hiss, cry, and storm in anger about the burial site.

Worms strove to crawl away.

Sleeping snakes slithered swiftly away.

Rats, warmly nested before, skittered precariously about the man's feet a moment, squeaking in alarm, and then fled into the darkness for safer harbor.

Then...

The ground erupted like a volcano bursting into life, sending a shower of burning debris high into the air.

Somewhere that night a constable looked up from his beat and thought a shooting star was passing. A straggler near the grave site road staggered away, crossing himself over and over, praying to God to protect him.

Dogs began barking for miles around.

Cats spit and cursed the air with claws and bites further yet.

Then, rising from the quicksand like burial ground, first a clenched fist scarred and leathery, then an arm with scrolls of tattoos upon it, then a head, grimacing and choking, spitting out years of dirt, vile fluids that had drenched his body at one time, and obnoxious festering creatures with multiple legs that sped swiftly down his chin back into the muck they had lived in before.

The rest of his body seemed to uncoil from his tomb like a viper from a piper's basket, until the miasma of fire and debris fell right left, front and back and the full towering height of Cyclops stepped forth.

He towered over the mysterious man who had freed him, an ancient one of old, a god reborn. His height was fearsome, but his face even more so! Bit as frightening a figure as this ancient god was, the man he stood before was the more worrisome. For he had no history of love or kindness. No brethren or loved ones long lost. He had only malice and anger, despair and hatred fueling his existence.

The short man did not shy from this giant. He fed upon its confusion and pain. Its vast loneliness and despair which were surging within its heart and threatening to overpower its newborn freedom. Mesmer's dark eyes glowed like those of a proud new father, who had just seen his child born, but his face was not filled with joy, hope and light, but instead with arrogance, anger, hatred, and darkness.

Cyclops stared into the eyes of the dread man who had called him forth.

"Why do you call me from the halls of Hades, mortal?" Cyclops demanded, his eyes blazing with long buried anger. Anger which has been distilled by many years of pain and suffering in the dark, miserable depths of Hade's halls.

He felt his body growing stronger by the minute and was prepared to destroy this mere mortal who dared to drag him from his death into this terrible world of light and dark, where mortals lived in the vane hopes of accumulating wealth and power, which inevitably must fade away, even as their pale, lackluster lives do.

Mesmer shocked Cyclops with his reply.

"No. It is not I who must answer you, but you me. What must you say? Answer me or surely, I will send you back into the grave from which I have risen you!"

Cyclops hated this man at once, wanted to rend him to pieces and hurl them as far away as possible, but he could not. How dare a mortal speak like that to a god. To a being of such immense power, he once could rend a mountain into rubble and raise a sea to drown a city.
But try as he might to resist this puny man, he felt this odd power holding him back, binding his arms to his sides.

Mesmer straightened, his eyes blazing now with fury and anger. "What must you call me?" He screamed; the rage of his dark soul so powerful that the land about him shook as if an earthquake had struck.

Cyclops trembled with rage, wanting to say many things that struck his miserable heart or what was left at that time, but instead all that came forth from between his parched lips was one simple word, which he would curse as long as he lived.

"Master!"

Epitaph for A Friend

Cute and fondly, soft as a tad,

His mother did hold him high

With good cheer and happy sighs

Warm with his dearest years.

But now as the zenith of his life

Do fade into Twilight

His memory alone is left

Glowing like a distant horizon

Sun lifting its eyes to peek

And bright our lives.

Their times scrolling in soft

Murmuring rainbows of Golden Light.

And he will not be forgotten.

Not his cloak.

His cape.

His pipe.

Or his wry grin.

This was and is not such a man

Who will be lost

At any cost.

His loss will be remembered

For generation after generation.

A shining star

In a world of darkness.

For his legacy is kindness

With manners so lightly worn,

Even his enemies held him in great esteem

As a man they feared and a man

Of fierce some deeds.

So farewell dear friend and companion,

Even to you the dearest to my heart

I must say farewell and goodbye.

But never will you wilt in the flower

Of my heart where you still grow

A part of me I was blessed to share.

No, you will stand there forever

In my heart

And theirs.

You will never part

Until our new lives dawn.

Then once again you will stand

Beside me as before

With cloak and pipe

A smile on your lips and say,

In your own inimical way,

"Come now, Dear Watson, the game is on,

Even here in Heaven's play."

    --Watson's epitaph for Sherlock Holmes

A Lesson Well Learned Soon Forgotten

"Sherlock, are you listening to me?"

Young Holmes snapped his attention at once from what he held in his hands and the vision he had just seen in his mind. The echo of loneliness and heartbreak he had heard in the words of the poem disturbed him to the core of his being. Even so, it did not cause him to lose attention to the world about him.

He was not that kind of person so easily distracted...by good, or bad.

He gave his full attention to the man asking. The Monk. A friend, scholar, and teacher.

Sherlock Holmes, a young man, nearing his twenties, hair still thick as a mop, fuzz on his chin and mustache faint as a woman's smile of laughter, twisted the braid of rope in his hands one more time and held it up.

"Sir, yes sir, I am."

The class turned to look.

Saw what he held up and broke into laughter.

The rope had been twisted and knotted until it resembled a human, both raggedy and forlorn, head drooping, arms straight out, but a feeling of loneliness exuding from it.

The Monk frowned. "Just what does a scarecrow have to do with what I have been teaching, Sherlock?"

Sherlock rose from the stiff woven cloth mat, which had spirals of mantric designs upon its face, and was but one of many such that the other students as well about him also sat upon.

They watched as he rose.

This was the afternoon session the Monk used to catch students up on lessons and impart new wisdom and questions for their eager minds to digest and dwell upon until understanding broke forth from the eggs of their confusion and gave life to a newly awakened understanding.

He stood off the mat in his bare feet, feeling the soothing cool of the veined marble floor the mat lay upon. It had not yet been freshly scrubbed, so the smell of salt and soiled feet lay heavy upon its surface, mostly ignored by the students, but for Sherlock, something he bore with fortitude, but most certainly was aware of.

Unlike many of the students, his senses, as long as he could remember were assaulted by levels of sensitivity none other seemed aware of. Curse or blessing he had not decided yet, though when he cleaned the latrines, he sometimes thought the latter.

Sherlock gave his fellow students a quick glance, then smiled at the Monk who sat in a lotus position, a saffron, orange robe surrounding his muscular body. His large eyes focused on Sherlock with a touch of amusement as he prepared to reply.

"A scarecrow is used by certain farmers in England, and much more so in the distant Americas, where they are used to frighten away the predators that might carouse through hard tilled fields and plunder them, leaving them with naught for the morrow to eat or to sell."

"Yes."

"And is also symbolic, for some, of the darker realms of man, wherein a soul gives up their best nature to carouse with that which is unthinkable or forbidden in rebellion against the Light of God."

The students muttered uneasily about him.

Sherlock went on. "Or as my friends here would say, Brahma, or perhaps Krishna of a more personal nature to believe in."

"And do you believe in God, Sherlock?" The Monk asked.

"I believe only that which my senses can detect."

"I see. And what of your higher senses."

"My third eye?"

His fellow students broke into laughter and poked at their foreheads.

"I do not speak of that which cannot be substantiated by others."

"Not all will believe you then?"

"No, Master. They will not. Which is why I will always rely on my senses and the logic of scientific deduction."

"Why?"

"Because when one lives in a world where most never look above five feet before them or three feet below, it is not smart to talk of anything that is above what they can see."

He paused a moment, then grinned. "Or below."

The students broke into laughter again.

"I see."

Sherlock eyed the Monk for a moment. Something had been nagging the back of his mind and now it stepped forth in all its glory. He smiled. He had thought he had been doing well; but he had let himself and his fellow students down by dwelling on the darker side briefly.

The very thing he had not wanted to do.

The Monk eyed him patiently, the hint of a smile on his lips. Almost as if he could read Sherlock's mind and followed his train of thoughts as Sherlock rode them.

"And yet…" Sherlock began, savoring what he knew he must say next. "And yet, a scarecrow is also a form of amusement for puppeteers, those who wish to refresh our spirits and bring us a certain joy, which even if only fleeting, brings some Light into our lives."

He looked around at his fellow students, who were watching him like hawks about to descend and tear his flesh apart. "And to show us what is finest in man's heart and spirt. Of that which Krishna and Buddha both taught in their teachings and in the West, Jesus the Christ!"

"I see," the Monk continued non-committedly. "Class dismissed."

The boys jumped up screaming happily, totally forgetting about Sherlock as they rushed outside to take in the afternoon hours of sunshine, still warming the bosom of Pahalgam, before the freezing flush of evening swept in the cooler Ganges breezes which forced them to remain indoors or suffer great chills and even worse, if they were sickly.

They all liked Sherlock, but he was too wordy and much too intellectual to their liking. So, sprinting forth from the room, they were like fish freshly being introduced to a new pond. They left hurriedly, scattering in every direction as fast as their whims and feet could carry them. No further thought of the lesson that the Monk had been trying to instill in them remained.

"Not you, Mister Holmes!" The Monk said sharply.

The few remaining students froze to look back.

The Monk gave them a stern look. "And you are also Holmes?"

They shook their heads and fled before he could say more.

Sherlock humbly waited to find out what his punishment was to be. Logically, it made no sense that he would be, but logic and Master were not always compatible he had discovered over the years he had spent with the Monk so far.

"Come!"

The Monk swept his saffron orange robes about him tightly, reached down and pulled up a long blanket made of gold thread and white silk threads. He quickly rolled the cloth up, then marched the opposite direction from the students.

Sherlock had no choice but to follow, his mind twisting and turning in what was more than likely a useless effort to understand what the Monk was up to. For he always, or at least most of the time, it seemed to Sherlock, to be on to something new. Sometimes exciting. Sometimes quite trying to young Sherlock's tender soul but always a lesson to be learned.

And that is precisely why he remained in this abode so far from his family and loved ones. He felt like a sponge in the presence of the Monk, hoping to soak up every nuance of the man's wisdom while he could.

"And soon forgotten!" The Monk would always say to Holmes later in jest. "You thirst for knowledge; and so quickly lose it."

But that was not entirely true. Holmes had a perfect memory. What the Monk was telling him was that facts alone were not enough. One had to marry facts with experience to make them worthy of remembering.

"This way!"

Sherlock scampered to catch up to the Monk, who though a good forty years or more older, seemed to have more energy than Sherlock's fellow students. Much more energy than an aged man approaching the zenith of his life.

They stepped through the kitchen, where the aromatic scents of spices, and boiling rice filled the air, ghee butter and chapattis being warmed and cooked in clay ovens, fresh yogurt and fruit being mixed and vegetable and fruit bowls being prepared by the young men who had not attended the lesson.

Their turn would come after the meal they were preparing.

Sherlock's turn to cook would come in the evening, which he preferred, because it gave him a chance to scamper off with the Monk and sit by the Ganges to listen to the wise man's tales of magic and mythology, truth, and wisdom.

They reached the back of the kitchen and exited to the grounds behind the large monastery. A series of tiled steps led from the back to a climbing path, which the Monk did not hesitate to ascend step by giant step.

Sherlock was genuinely curious now. He had been told by his fellow students that the man rarely traveled this way. But when the Monk did those who went with him never spoke afterwards of what happened. Of what they saw or experienced.

That both terrified and entranced Sherlock. He hoped for further enlightenment but feared sometimes that the unknown of this Monk's life might be too terrible for him to understand.

But he was wrong as usual. The Monk was a book of many pages, each paragraph delicately written, but each word selected, powerful and demanding, sucking Holmes's intellectual curiosity further and further. It terrified Holmes sometimes afterwards, that he felt so powerless with the Monk. But the fear and terror did not come because of darkness in the Monk's soul, but the darkness the Monk exposed in the souls of others, as he gently prodded them towards the Light.

As Sherlock followed, he was increasingly curious where this path with its gigantic stone steps led, and what manner of man would require such large steps. Or if it had even been a man who had carved and walked these steps!

Logic dictated that a giant had built these steps; but Sherlock had learned all too well by now that logic was not something you could easily get away with when a Master was concerned.

The Monk, most definitely a Master, was daunting and delightful, kind but fierce. Forgiving but demanding. But always, his actions led to logic and truth, never to anything that was less than the best for anyone he helped or taught.

But as far as Sherlock could make of the Monk, he seemed hellbent on twisting reality about like string on a finger to confuse a young mind and to force it to blossom with new understanding...like it or not.

But as he sighed inwardly at how effortlessly the Monk climbed ahead of him, as if many years younger, Sherlock had to suck in more air to keep up. He felt like an old man as he followed the Monk. He realized it was the "not," that attracted him the most to the Monk's revelations. Not what he, Sherlock, understood as reality, but what he did not understand. And was soon proven to be a much greater truth than he had looked for!

Londonderry Market

The front door chimed the musical notes of a simple Mozart tune as it was opened and shut. The tinkling of the chime silvered the air with a cheery welcoming feeling, but what passed through the open doorway, was not cheering at all.

It was a shadow, glanced at the corner of the eye. Moving slowly through the front aisle of the market, but no one seemed to notice its passing, nor the man who made it. It was like those shadows we see passing swiftly past us on the right or left, or even in front of us, that we cannot quite grasp the significance of whether it is a palpable living being or not.

A ghost.

A mirage.

Who knows?

The mind can play tricks. Associating certain emotions, even past events of terror with current tricks of the eye can fool the mind into thinking something that is not, exist. But in this case, the opposite is the case.

The shadow is a thief of recognition, a masked entity of humanity long past its time of certain identity on our world, a creature of nightmares and fancy. And as such, it stalks past rows of fresh potatoes, tomatoes, lettuce, cabbage, and oranges and apples, fresh bread on shelves wrapped in soft cloth, but still warm, their scent fragrancing the air with a tasty aroma that instantly makes most customers hungry, even when they are not.

All good chefs and cooks know that the fragrance your food emits can magnetize a person's interest or repel it with just one added element, or odd pick of spice or scent.

But in this case the fresh breads are like capable surgeons. Able to dissect our fancies. Array them in different, tasty fragrances that water the mouth. Tease our imagination, sending floods of shivers up and down taste buds. The recognition brought by the fairy of flavor begins taunting our senses with visions of fresh toast, buttered rolls, and French bread laden with butter...garlic sauce and fresh marmalade for breakfast. Or dipped in thick brown lamb sauce or stew in the evening.

Yes, this is a store that brings back, not only memories of delightful meals, but present ones to come and hopefully continue coming long into a future we cannot even begin to imagine, but hope will be there.

Then the shadowy form makes a slight turn towards the back where Mister Stickelberry, the son of Mister and Ms. Stickelberry, who was himself the son of a Stickelberry, is excited, thinking another live customer has come to sample his masterpieces.

He is a third-generation grocer who grew up in the trade and wished nothing different from his earliest of days of emerging from a diaper into toddler clothing and later britches, short suits, and pants. Baking and groceries were his life. His blood.

"Sir? May I help you?" He asks, without truly looking at to whom he is speaking. A mistake. He might yet have had a chance were he to look up. But he did not.

The shadow paused before the back counter where Mister Stickelberry, a stout man with a waddle of chin beard that made him look comical but added generously to the humorous look of his eyes. Eyes which always crinkled in some form of smile, even when his lips did not follow the gesture, or his cheeks.

He wiped at his nose. It had been running the last hour. *Must be a cold* he thought and ignored it, as he did most physical things. *The body is weak, but the spirit is strong* his father always reminded him when he wanted to stay home from school or...from work, which turned out to be every day of the following years. But over time, he found the routine to be something he had grown fond of. And it prepared him for the day and the evening, which brought its own challenges and rewards at home with his family.

"Sir?" He squawked awkwardly as his eyes finally landed on the shadowy form that had reached him.

The shadowy form was made up of a moldy looking overcoat and long gloves that reeked of mold and decay. Atop its head was a wide brimmed top hat, which had seen too many years of wear. So many that it looked fresh from a graveyard. The shape looked at Mister Stickelberry.

The terror that gripped Mister Stickelberry was unknown to him before this moment. Not even his childhood nightmares could have prepared him for this meeting. Nor would it have!

Especially when the substance of the shadowy form, flesh, dried and leathery, like from an old tomb, moved closer and with vacuous eyes that glowed as if by a distant lamp inside the skull, searched his frightened ones and then spoke three powerful words.

"I'm for you."

An Unexpected Turn of Events

The tone of the monster's voice, the shape of the being before him chilled Mister Stickelberry to the very center of his soul, but he braved it out, even managing a weak smile.

"Indeed. Most here are for me. I am the grocer. And a dratted good one, even if I say so my..."

He choked out the word "Self!" Because he was like a car left with the motor running, words spilling out, while his brain and heart were elsewhere, hoping to somehow find a way out...escape...but knowing there was none.

A leathery hand, veined with green lines and strings of flesh shot from the moldy sleeve of the monstrous being's overcoat and grabbed him by the throat.

Mister Stickelberry's eyes began to pop forth from their sockets as the air was blocked from reaching his lungs. He felt the strength draining from his legs for the lack of oxygen and began to sag, but the hand kept him upright, choking further and further.

He made choking sounds, strong at first, then weaker as his lungs emptied entirely. Mister

Stickelberry's thoughts were no longer escape, but now memories of his family and the mistakes he had made, that now were too late to fix. He despaired, even as he felt the numbness from his dangling legs, kicking in the air, no longer there.

He finally was able to focus on the being killing him and found himself looking into the eyes of hell itself. He saw no escape, no redemption. Only a dark and terrible end of days.

The last thing he saw before he passed entirely into the next world, was a bright tunnel of light blossoming forth to embrace him.

Death's Call

Mister Stickelberry did not hear the screams of customers who fled the building, more concerned for their own lives now that they had become aware of the giant who held Mister Stickelberry in the air as easily as a father might his baby.

The screams of the fleeing customers tore the afternoon airs, frightening those on the sidewalks outside on both sides of the street. The sounds of terror added to the fear and confusion that was building in the hearts of those outside. In desperation to get away from what was driving the others out in terror, men and women fought to get away, flooding into the street like a powerful, agitated tide on the ocean's shore. Bodies fell and were walked upon. Others fell into the dirty gutters, while still more stormed like an angry floodwater into the street.

Mothers wrapped arms about their babies and children and dropped into protective huddles against the push of the bodies.

Brakes screamed. Horses cried out in fright and raised on their rear legs, spilling passengers, overturning carriages. Even the newer Tesla powered electric cars and older Steam powered ones with the huge propellers thrusting them forward found themselves in a storm of trouble they could not avoid.

They slammed on their brakes to avoid hitting the panicked population. But too late for some pedestrians, who were struck powerfully by the iron metal of bumpers and sides, then flung high into the air, and slammed into buildings and parked vehicles and carriages.

It was a scene of massive terror and carnage.

Moments later, Mister Stickelberry burst through the shop windows, hurtling like a missile of flesh and blood into the air, shedding flesh, bone, and blood as he smashed into the opposite side of the street against the neighboring garment store, where the finest of ladies took their leisure, shopping the latest trends from Paris and Moscow.

Today was not a good shopping day.

Neither for clothing, or for groceries and fine, fresh loaves of bread. The only meal that would be served this day would be death and the only clothing a cloak of horror and soul tearing terror.

Two constables came running at the sound of blaring horns, screaming men and women, and the crash of broken glass and twisting, tortured metal bumpers.

What they found left of Mister Stickelberry was hardly enough for his grieving widow to gather into a coffin for a proper Christian burial later. In fact, to do so, it took a full squad of constables most of the afternoon and into the night to find all his body parts and for the local street cleaners to mop up, wash down, soap, clean and disinfect the nearest of buildings that had been affected and the street on both sides, as well as the sidewalks.

It would be the talk of London for a long time.

Until the second time it happened.

"I find this quite chilling," Watson declared as he threw the morning London times down on the table and rose to face Holmes, who had been quietly reading beside the fireplace, a lap blanket warming him.

What Watson had read turned his stomach; and he normally has quite a strong one. Being a doctor and a much in demand one at times, he should have felt no discernible upset from what he had read, but his imagination, far more vivid than reality and based in the science he knew and practiced left him feeling sick in his soul. He even left uneaten the remaining sweet cherry scone laying on his breakfast plate.

And not much in this world or the next ones could easily pry the good doctor away from his favorite dessert!

"And disgusting! Very, very disgusting!" He spit out, as if the words would cleanse his soul of what he had read. And hopefully, settle the bile rising into his throat. "I don't know what London is coming to these days," he complained.

Holmes looked up from the tome in his hands. "That makes two of us, my dear Watson." He set aside his lap blanket, set down the tome on the chair, then the blanket over it. "I think we have a case, Watson."

"Think or know?" Watson asked with a forced smile. He was praying it was not what he had just read about. Please, please dear God, he prayed. But some prayers are not answered as we all too often realize. Sometimes what we pray for is not the path chosen for us. And this was such a time.

Holmes did not reply. He went to the coat rack for his cape and cap, then slipped a pistol from a cabinet and stuffed it into his jacket and headed for the stairs.

Watson arched an eyebrow questioningly, then noticed the book's cover and the title of which Holmes had been glancing through.

Legendary giants.

That caused him to raise both eyebrows in surprise. What did a giant have to do with the recent death? Now, the poor man, felt not only nauseated, but a cold chill freezing his soul.

Watson hurriedly got up to follow Holmes. He grabbed his coat and hat, clinging to the familiar to chase away those feelings now gnawing at his usually cheery nature. He sighed unhappily, but followed Holmes downstairs, where he found the man greeting Professor Challenger and Conan, both dressed as if going for an outing, rather than arrived for a personal visit.

"Watson!" Conan greeted and shook his hand.

Challenger smiled. "You're coming with us, of course?"

"With you? But I and Holmes are on a case now…"

"As are we all," Conan chirped in delightedly.

"Agreed!" Challenger growled with a smile.

Watson glanced at Holmes, surprise clouding his features. "I thought we had a new case."

"We do. Come, I will explain on the way over. Our ride should be here shortly."

The honk of a car.

Watson and the others turned to look as a police wagon stopped out front by the curb.

Constable Evans looked out at them with a smile. "Anyone need a ride?"

The young man with the huge mop of red hair looked just like his father, Inspector Bloodstone, and he never acted as a taxi driver, except on the rare occasion when his father was on a rare case that demanded swift action.

In this case, the gathering of Holmes and his friends.

The Second Crime Scene

Challenger watched as Holmes and Watson went over the clues of the crime scene. Ropes connected to wooden stands surrounded the area of the incident. Watson noted that the ropes extended almost an entire city block.

The spider web of ropes stretched all four directions of the Holy Cross as the intersection of Wayne, Myers, Croft and Krumbly was cheerfully named by some devoted worshippers at the nearby church.... named, Holy Cross.

The Holy Cross is one of the largest and most prominent of downtown London crossways, whereby traffic over the London Bridge and traffic from the outermost boroughs of London converged with tourists coming to view Buckingham Palace, hoping to catch a glimpse of Good Queen Mary, and soldiers enroute to the Thames docks where the great propeller warships, afloat above their watery brothers, waited for them to board for the latest incursion into the Dark China Isles, where a recent outburst of murder and magic had flamed to life.

Conan and Challenger exchanged glances. They remembered quite well the unholy chap who had brought forth the first alarm of discomfort from that area of the world. Mesmer!

"I don't like what I see, Challenger."

"Curse that man who will not die!" Conan uttered.

"Really, Conan? Curse? You hardly seem the sort who would resort to such a lowly manner of action."

"I am not, but that monster deserves the worst."

"I do not wish him better either. But a curse would make us no different than that monster was. Were he repentant I might be persuaded to forgive, but that is not likely. So, for now, Conan, let us be calm about it all and see what Holmes and Watson are up to. Holmes never requests our attention unless it is something he feels we can help with."

Conan shivered. "Right now, he could help us by providing some hot tea!"

Challenger smiled. Took a flask from his right jacket pocket and held it up. "Will this do?"

"You're a man after my own heart." Conan accepted the flask.

Challenger returned his attention to Watson as he handed Holmes a new vial, which Holmes used to scoop some fleshy matter off the wall of the flower shop window, where it had struck and slid down to the brick windowsill, perched there like some obscene creature waiting to leap at its next victim.

"Happy Sunshine," Challenger muttered. He only wished it were...happy sunshine...but he kept his black thoughts about the horror to a quip at best.

Conan handed back the flask. Challenger took it and did a long swig of his own.

"What's wrong?"

"Defiling a flower shop window is disgraceful."

"Why do you say that?"

"It is like rape. A thing of beauty deserves respect, not torture."

Conan was about to comment, when Watson glanced at them, then at the vial in Holmes' hand.

"Disgusting!" Watson growled. He was angry because he was exactly where he had hoped he would not be. Drat it all!

"Quite!" Challenger agreed.

Conan and Challenger both stepped closer to eye the contents of the vial. "It looks alive somehow."

He glanced at Conan. "Is that possible?"

Conan eyed Watson, who shuddered. "Not unless

flesh can come alive on its own without consciousness to enlighten it."

Holmes said nothing, his eyes had discovered something far more interesting than commenting upon an obvious state of being. "Come here, old chaps."

They followed him.

Watson stepped to Holmes right when he stopped and Challenger and Conan to the left to look at something on a rain gutter pipe which descended from the roof above. The gutter was rusty, weather worn and pockmarked. Obviously, it had not been cleaned in some time, as the dirt stains, soot and rust made for the perfect medium to capture a rather large handprint prominently made upon it. There had been a fresh rain the night before and it had caused an overflow of muck which formed a muddy trail. It resembled a decaying slime monster, freshly dripping along the ductwork, forming icicles of reddish muck which seemed alive in a dark and horrid fashion.

Conan cringed. His stomach was protesting so loudly, he was sure anyone could hear it. His face was pale and sickly at that moment. "I knew I shouldn't have had eggs for breakfast."

Challenger laughed. "Imagine that. A queasy doctor."

"See here!" Watson exclaimed, holding a magnifying glass over the handprint. The same swishy substance captured in one of the vials Holmes had secured squirmed lifelike beneath the clarity of the magnifying glass.

"It's definitely disgusting," Challenger noted. "But Holmes, we've seen worse."

"Far!" Holmes agreed.

Watson took a sample into a new vial and was just, shutting his black medical bag, he always carried with him, when Challenger let out a loud exclamation of surprise.

"I say!" Challenger growled.

"Mind yourself, Challenger!" Holmes demanded as he placed Challenger's right hand just barely over the giant handprint.

"I can feel that drudge below me moving. Must I?"

"Indeed, you must!" Holmes replied. "Just don't touch it!" He warned.

Challenger jerked his hand free, then took a deep breath and placed it again over the handprint, but this time a tad further away.

"See here, Watson. What do you think?"

Watson eyed the size of the handprint and Challenger's hand over it. "He's a giant."

"I am not a giant," Challenger angrily declared.

"Not you, oaf, the handprint is of a giant," Watson explained irritably.

"Through?" Challenger demanded.

Holmes nodded.

Challenger quickly cleaned the palm of his hand with a handkerchief. He began to automatically put it back into his suit pocket, then thought better and tossed the handkerchief into the muck beneath his foot, where he added a boot and heel to make sure anything alive on it, would not stay so.

"It never touched you, Challenger," Conan teased.

"Then put your hand over it and tell me how it feels!" Challenger growled angrily.

Conan started to, then smiled. "I'll trust in your judgement on this."

"Thought so!" Challenger announced loudly, as if he were in a theater instead of next to his friend.

Holmes and Watson exchanged glances, but neither spoke up.

"Very large indeed," Holmes finally commented.

He glanced at Challenger, who had lost his angry scowl upon Conan's retreat and smiled benevolently at Conan. "The handprint reminds me of that man from Mars we met once."

"Ah, Carson Carter," Holmes acknowledged. "On Mars, a Thakoor's hand is as big as the doorway we stand next to."

Watson groaned. "Please, don't remind me!"

Conan glanced at him.

"You were not here at that time, Conan. You were still on the other Earth."

"Oh."

Challenger gave Conan a gloating look. "You would have loved that case. We got to get our arses nearly chewed off by six-legged lizards the size of elephants and shot and sliced by triple barreled long guns and double slice swords with jagged teeth."

"Quite fun I suppose," Conan remarked cheerily.

Challenger ignored him, then eyed Holmes "What manner of creature on this world could possibly leave a handprint that size, I wonder," he mused, eyes on Holmes, who was listening intently to the conversation.

"What do you believe, Conan?" Holmes asked.

"Definitely some kind of malformed human creature. Suffering from giantism, no doubt." Conan turned to Watson.

"I concur that is a possibility. However," Watson looked doubtful. "I've never seen such a hand with curved fingernails that resemble claws."

"Claws?" Challenger inquired in surprise.

Watson used a pair of tweezers to carefully pry away a leaf that had become attached to the lower part of the handprint.

It revealed a heavily indented area. "Yes, most definitely claws."

Challenger shuddered.

Holmes nodded. "Very good, Watson. I saw the same thing on the poor dead man's neck as well."

Challenger growled deeply in his throat. "Unfortunately, so have I."

"What?" Conan demanded. "You know what did this then?"

Holmes and the others eyed Challenger.

"Not what, but who!" He frowned deeply, plucked out his handkerchief to wipe away sudden sweat on his brows. "And not so much a who...as a what...or more properly...described. Something not human at all."

Holmes nodded.

Challenger seemed to be encouraged by the motion. "When I visited the Arboreal Plateau in Africa, near the portal that divides our world from that of Fairie, I ran into a certain creature…I say creature…because he was less human and more a cunning, predator."

"How so?" Watson asked, surprised by the description.

"He suffered from giantism as you call it, but was not malformed in any way, except for one."

"Yes?" Holmes asked. "Please do continue."

"I cannot. Even today, after all these years, it gives me nightmares to think of him."

Holmes nodded. "Did he have a name?"

"He did. And one I suspect he chose to mock us normal humans."

"Cyclops."

Everyone turned to look at Holmes in surprise.

Holmes smiled. "Watson, surely you examined the book I was reading before you left."

Watson nodded. "But I thought it was merely legendary and not factual."

"It was both."

"How so?"

"There is a legend that runs through many of the more ancient tribal civilizations of our world of a demi-god who once walked the Earth. He was one of many, though humans turned on the monsters and eventually only one remained. And he was defeated by a Greek sailor."

"Odysseus!" Challenger roared.

Conan chuckled. "Oh God! Why do the evil ones get to live so long?"

Holmes smiled. "I wouldn't be so quick to mock this one. He is for real."

"Like Frankenstein?" Inspector Bloodstone growled, joining them with his look-a-like son, Constable Evans, who gave the muck a closer look, then raised a pale face to look at them.

Watson put a hand on his shoulder. "You'll get over it, Constable Evans."

"Constable, you all, right?" Holmes inquired kindly. "You seem a bit pale."

"The muck here reminds me of why I now have come to speak with you. I found the dead person's head."

"I see."

"Head?" Challenger roared. "But Holmes, you said you examined the poor fellow's neck."

Holmes shrugged. "The neck remained."

The stomach lurches that had been bothering Conan finally reached a critical moment. He made gagging sounds, clamped a hand over his mouth and rushed way.

"Poor Conan!" Challenger sighed.

Holmes dropped the topic. He glanced at Watson, who nodded. "I'll look into it, Holmes."

He started to leave, then hesitated.

"Do not worry, Watson, you need not worry over the killer at this point. He has been fed."

Watson bit back his reply, knowing that Holmes would not explain anyway, but still shuddered. It was hard for him to deal with it rationally now, so instead he suppressed the sudden fear building in his gut and glanced at Constable Evans. "Shall we?"

Constable Evans sucked in a deep breath, nodded, and led Watson away. Both men were doing their best to keep the contents of their stomachs down at that moment, though for quite distinct reasons. Both glanced at Conan as they passed him, his head over a garbage can.

"Conan, want to see the head of the poor merchant who died with us?"

Conan looked up, gripping the garbage can to hold himself steady. "Head? I thought…"

Conan put two and two together and throw his head into the can again to throw up further.

The Killer's Identity

"So, what do we have here?" Inspector Bloodstone demanded, perhaps a bit too gruffly, but considering it was his basic nature to be gruff, no surprise to Conan, Challenger and Holmes.

Holmes cocked a neutral eye on the Inspector, who withered somewhat beneath Holmes' gaze. Sherlock Holmes was the only man he could never look square in the eye and feel comfortable. "I brought my friends for very important reasons, Inspector."

"Those being?" Demanded Inspector Bloodstone, ignoring the intimidation he felt from Holmes, perhaps even a bit more annoyed because he felt it weighing him down like a ton of bricks. Of his own making surely, but all the same, extremely uncomfortable.

Challenger growled angrily, not liking the Inspector's tone. "Inspector, I am the only man here who has seen the killer you are going to be looking for."

Everyone gave Challenger a surprised look, but Inspector Bloodstone. He merely arched an eyebrow appraisingly. "And who might that be, Professor?"

"Cyclops," Challenger replied, choking on the words as he spoke to them.

Conan put a comforting hand on his friend's arm.

"Thanks, Conan. I am fine. It is just that name brings up so many unhappy memories I would have preferred never to experience again."

Challenger eyed the Inspector. "You know the name, of course."

"I do not."

"I assure you, that if it is indeed Cyclops, as all indications point to, if you do not know him yet, you soon shall."

Holmes perked up. His surprise when he concluded a series of deductions, based on witness accounts, historical events, and now the actual physical clues were all coming together quite nicely. He would have preferred they not. But science is science and facts are facts. "This...Cyclops...you believe him to be the killer. Why?"

Challenger shook his head. "Not in the manner which our Inspector here would consider a killer to be." Challenger reddened in embarrassment, "Nor in a manner, which you are accustomed to either Holmes. If he is the one. And I do believe him to be, then this case has been brought to another level of complication than it already is."

"Drat it all, Challenger. You are beginning to vex me like Holmes here with your vague assertions. What kind or killer is he?" The Inspector demanded.

Challenger shut his eyes.

The Inspector felt suddenly as if the air had become chilled and shivered. "Speak up, man, you're terrifying me!"

Challenger opened his yes. "I can't tell you."

"What can you tell me then?"

Challenger eyed Holmes. "I know you, Holmes, you have been playing coy about what you know. Perhaps you could share what I see in your eyes that you already suspect...or know?"

Holmes nodded and turned to the Inspector, who was nervously pulling on the ends of his red, walrus shaped mustache, causing its bright fiery ruby ends to become bruised and dark from the dirt on his fingers

"The man we are more than likely seeking is not the giant."

Inspector Bloodstone cursed beneath his breath, then hissed angrily. "For God's sake, Holmes, quite beating around the busy and just tell us!"

Holmes smiled, then told them.

The Giant Stone

After Sherlock and the Monk had been climbing for what seemed like hours, the Monk finally slowed as the last of the giant stones of the staircase path vanished, its last stone half buried in dirt and bright yellow and gold leafed philodendron, which thrust bright pointed leaves in many directions as they clustered in thick bunches against the sides of the new path, which was a smooth grassy sward that lead between giant, upright stones.

Also, clutching the edges of the stones on both sides were thick spear moss, laced with fresh green leafy vines and spots of white and red stone flowers, a rare species only found in the Himalayas and especially Pahalgam.

They stepped onto the narrow path, the philodendron grasping their ankles where it had overgrown the narrow walkway.

The Monk made a face. "I need to have someone come here and clean this up; it's not proper."

"Someone by the name of Sherlock?" Sherlock asked, a smile teasing his lips, causing his eyes to dance with amusement.

The Monk laughed and clapped a hand on his student's right shoulder. "I haven't even begun to teach you any courses in mind reading and yet here you are, reading my very thoughts."

They both laughed.

The Monk returned his attention to their path and began walking again.

"Just a bit further now."

The low-lying flowers, fern, moss, and plants gave way to taller shrubbery then an overhead like arch of twisted wood that opened into a final path towards something huge that began filling Sherlock's vision.

"What is that?"

The Monk remained silent.

Finally, they cleared the arch and came out the other side.

Sherlock paused, mouth hanging open.

Rising like something out of a Greek fantasy was a huge hand. It was massive and carved from various stones that had been interwoven together to give it the appearance of fancy Indian carvings or fancy pieces of jewelry imported from the Chinas.

"Stunning, is it not, Sherlock?"

The Monk sat in a half lotus position before the huge hand and put his hands together in the symbol of Namaste...a recognition of the Godhood in each man and woman of our world and a token of peace and goodwill. "Peace be unto the past. Peace be unto the present. Peace be unto the future."

Sherlock sat next to him.

"What is this...this...?"

The Monk smiled. "I was speechless too the first time I found it."

"Found?" He gave the Monk a surprised look.

"Only a very, very few know of this statue. And fewer still of what it means."

Sherlock nodded. "It's magical?"

"You can sense that, can you?"

"Yes." Sherlock eyed the Monk, a twinkle in his eyes. "But not the kind of magic that a circus clown, or stage magician would boast as such."

The Monk smiled. "Yes, true magic. Magic of the spirit. God's energies."

"But many would find this image quite frightening, would they not?"

"Yes. But only because they see with the eyes of their fears and not the tender joy and love of their heart."

He turned to Holmes. "Never forget the true magic, Sherlock."

He touched a forefinger to Holmes's chest over his heart. "Never!"

He was silent a long moment, then added. "A man who keeps in touch with the Divine Spirit inside will never be alone, never be lost to the world and more importantly will never lose his way."

"His way?" Sherlock asked.

The Monk did not answer. Instead, he shut his eyes and began to meditate.

Sherlock puzzled by the prior statement, pondered its meaning a few moments, then his face lit up.

He now understood what the Monk meant by his way. It was precisely why he had come to India to study and to learn. Because he felt that in England, he was losing the way before him.

He sighed with relief.

That moment brought a huge release for him. A weight of intellectual doubt lifted from his shoulders and his decision to leave his friends and family to come here no longer weighted him down. He felt as free as the eagles who soared the heights.

He shut his eyes and began to meditate, allowing himself to find the way within himself that all can find if only they care to do so.

He felt his breathing slow, then his pulse, and finally the excitement of his discovery and self-revelation lessened and he settled into a deep silence. One with which a man or woman can know true peace and contentment.

Challenger sighed. "A demigod."

"You're saying that this killer, this monster…" Inspector Bloodstone almost choked out. "That he's a demi-god?"

"Yes."

Conan, who had staggered back, pale, and weak, rejoined them. He overheard the last of the conversation and shook his head. "The God I worship would never do such a thing to another being."

"That's because the God you worship is one of love and compassion," Holmes explained. "But these demi-gods, they are fallen from the grace of God and have chosen a darker path."

"Are you talking fallen angels?" Conan gasped, shocked at the analogy Holmes had spoken.

"Darker path?" The Inspector repeated.

"Indeed. And this one, the one that Challenger finds quite distressing. He is one of the worst." Holmes turned to Conan. "And no, he is not a fallen angel. He is merely a being of immense power who has lost their way."

Holmes paused a moment, to collect his thoughts, and clarify what he knew. "An incredibly famous Greek sailor

met this one and others like him."

Challenger got it right away. "A cyclops. You are telling me we are dealing with a ten-foot tall, one eyed, horn-headed cyclops?"

Watson frowned. "Are they not supposed to be giants?"

"No, Challenger and yes, dear Watson, they are. At least compared to the much shorter men of the Grecian era," Holmes explained.

"Men were much shorter then than now. Though this one might have been thought a giant in his own time, now he is merely tall and frightening."

"But how can you know that just from a book?" Watson demanded.

"Not from the book, but from what we have discovered. And which you two, Conan and Watson, will no doubt prove effortlessly once you analyze the samples we have gathered in the Cold Room. Holmes turned to Inspector Bloodstone. "Of course, with your approval, Inspector."

"You have it."

"There, they shall confirm your and my deepest fears."

"Which are?"

"That he has been summoned back into our world once more to do mischief."

"Summoned?" Inspector Bloodstone growled. "But if he is a god, why would he need to be summoned back? And by what?"

"Not by what, but by whom, Inspector."

"But why would a god need the help of a man to come forth?"

"Demi-god, Inspector. Dependent upon the energies of man to survive. The earliest of magics, which I am sure that our dear friend Harry Houdini would acknowledge, is that of faith and belief. The earliest man believed in these beings and gave them existence."

Watson nodded. "More than likely through ignorance and fear. Even were they not magical in some way, the fact of their size and distorted features would be enough to shake up a man's soul and give rise to superstitious nonsense. "Look how long our dear friend, Frankenstein, the so-called monster, was persecuted because of his looks and size. And he never claimed to be anything, but a soul caught in a stew of dead men's bodies."

Holmes glanced at Watson. "Watson, that's rather poetic of you."

Watson blushed. "I do read other things than the journals I write about you, Holmes." Watson nodded to Holmes and left the group.

Challenger grinned at the warmth that Holmes an Watson shared. It made him feel good about a world that was often hard and cold. Challenger nodded. "Indeed. In my journeys I learned that, at one time, many Cyclops existed. Their lands were near that of Circe. But this one...Cyclops...he has a penchant for flesh and violence. It is rumored in legend that he was cast from heaven."

"Why?"

"Inspector. Rumors and myths, legends are all but grains of sand on the seashore of truth. I can only conjecture."

Holmes nodded. "But we do know this. The like of this demi-god, Cyclops, or unusual human more than likely, has not ever been seen in London."

"That is true," the Inspector agreed. "I'd have known of it, were that so."

"And two, no man's hand is that large, not even that of Frankenstein!"

"And his is quite large indeed," Conan agreed.

"But he's a good man," Challenger interjected.

"Yes. And a friend," Holmes added. "Inspector, we also know, and I believe Watson and Conan here will confirm soon, that what we discovered is not just flesh, but an amalgamation."

"You mean like a golem?" The Inspector spit out, feeling bile rising to his throat after he said it.

Holmes replied by looking at Challenger, whose face had grown paler than before.

"Challenger?" The Inspector demanded. "What do you have to say of this?"

"Golem."

A deathly silence fell over the lot of them.

A police wagon pulled to the side of the alley and Watson hollered out its window. "Holmes, we're ready!"

Holmes turned to the Inspector. "I'll leave you and your good men to wrap this up now."

"I'll join you as soon as we have,"

Holmes nodded.

He went to the police wagon and climbed inside, followed by Challenger and Conan.

The Inspector eyed the handprint again. A large cockroach was making its way sluggishly down the slime of the pipe and reached the handprint. It stepped into it and then began making struggling motions, its deep brown body dissolving and eating away.

The Inspector could not stand it.

He took his pistol out and used its butt to smash it to death, putting the bug out of its misery.

Then he tossed his weapon to the ground. It fell into the muck at the base of the drain, where the ooze from the handprint drained onto it.

He watched in horror and fascination as the weapon gradually dissolved into acrid swirls of smoke.

"Demi-gods!" He growled in disgust and strut out of the alley like an offended peacock ready to do battle.

As constables came rushing to meet him, he ordered. "Do not touch what you find. It must be cleaned at a distance and once thoroughly cleaned, then burned and buried deeply."

Londonderry Market

Challenger stood on the rooftop, looking down, Conan on the opposite building's roof. "Holmes."

Holmes looked up from the sidewalk, where he had been gathering samples.

"You should see this."

Rooftop

"There!"

Holmes followed the direction of Challenger's gesture and frowned.

"You're sure?"

Conan joined them, huffing, and puffing. "I saw the same thing at the flower shop."

Holmes frowned.

He looked at the two. "You must hurry back to the Inspector and make sure he joins me with armed constables."

"You can't go there alone!" A shocked Challenger cried out.

Holmes ignored him.

He was already slipping over the side of the building on its fire escape.

"I hate it when he does that!" Challenger growled.

Challenger hollered down at Holmes. "Where are you off to now?"

"To meet an old friend. Tell Watson to look for a giant fist."

"A what?" Challenger roared.

But Holmes was already out of sight and hearing.

The Black Goddess

The salty air of the Thames was both nippy and rejuvenating to Holmes as he stepped onto the docks to survey the merchant ships that bobbed gently up and down, held firm by their moorings.

It did not take Holmes long to find the ship he had seen from the Londonderry Market. Its flag was all too obvious. A giant statute of a fist.

The same one he had seen in Pahalgam.

Holmes stood in the shadows of a large stack of wooden containers. Yet to added to the lower decks of t he hold of the merchant ship. The shadow of a giant head fell across the front of the containers, then the top of a head, wearing a huge sailor's cap rose into view. A face briefly turned Holmes's direction, but the eyes glanced in another direction and missed him.

Holmes' suspicions were confirmed at once. This was the one who had left the huge handprint. He backed deeper into the shadows of the wooden containers, their brine-tainted wood stained. Exuding a faint odor of salt and pepper. Used to carry metal buckets of the condiments for the potatoes, which kept sailors from getting scurvy. Which made for quite an interesting aroma, combined with the sweaty salt spray that had, also, tainted the containers.

He felt a presence behind him.

"Don't turn around."

Holmes stiffened.

"Doctor Mesmer, I presume. Quite clever how you have managed to fake your death so you could return at a more auspicious time…when all thought you dead."

"A good plan I must admit."

"Plan for what?"

"You are an intelligent man, Holmes. Need I spell it out to the last letter for you?"

"What is your plan, Mesmer? If it is revenge, you have the wrong people."

"I think that you are too smart for that sort of nonsense, knowing the powers I hold now."

"And if you thought that you would be right."

A chuckle. "I see you haven't lost your sense of humor."

Holmes turned around.

Mesmer stood behind him, his right hand extended, a dangerous black glow shining forth from his fingers and palm. "I could kill you easily."

"But that would be boring, would it not?"

Mesmer smiled. "Yes. Very. And not nearly as long as would make me happy."

Holmes felt a pair of hands grip his shoulders and he was elevated several feet off the planks beneath him.

Mesmer smiled. "I'd like to introduce you to someone, Mister Holmes."

"I've already been introduced, as have several of his victims."

"He may be less inclined to favor a bit of humor before tearing your soul forth from your body."

Holmes was revolved slowly in the giant's hands so they were face to face. It took but a moment for him to know the rest of his deductions were also correct.

The eyes of the man before him, were not those of an arrogant, cannibalistic god, but of a small child, looking, searching for affection and finding nothing but pain and sorrow..

Mesmer smiled. "Would like you to meet a dear friend of mine."

Holmes smiled into the giant's face, as if meeting an old friend. "Cyclops, I presume? How good to finally meet you."

Cyclops cocked his head. Surprised. "Good?"

"Why yes. I would love to hear more about your life, when you are free to do so, of course."

"Why?"

Holmes's eyes sparkled with energy. What he said next, he meant with his heart. "Because I believe you could teach me much about this world's history. One can never know enough."

Cyclops pulled Holmes closer to his face to search the detective's eyes. "You lie!"

"No. I would never do that with a good man like you."

"I am not...good."

"In God's eyes, all men are good. Even those who have lost their way for a time."

Mesmer exploded, seeing what Holmes was doing. And it was working. He screamed. "Take him away. Now, Cyclops! I order you!"

Cyclops frowned at Mesmer a long time, but then noted Mesmer's fists were swirling with black energies. So, he nodded instead.

"I obey!"

Cyclops threw Holmes over his right shoulder like you might a man who was drowning. Then he went up the boarding ramp. As he did, Holmes caught a clear glimpse of a second flag, which hidden by the other at first. It was black colored, with bold red letters that proclaimed, "The Black Goddess."

"Yes. My ship."

"Hard to believe that Mesmer would name a ship after a demi-god."

"He did not. I did," Cyclops said.

"Why?"

Cyclops looked away, his eyes half shut, clearly a lot of things that had been bothering him before, were now boiling to the surface with the introduction of Holmes into his life.

But, used to abuse and loneliness, he withheld his feelings and instead of being honest about what was bothering him, he said, "Because."

Holmes was put on a wooden chair that had seen better days. Only three legs. But the chair was nailed through its back to the sea wall of the hold. Cyclops held Holmes steady with one giant hand, and with the other would a rope, already about the chair tightly about Holmes's chest.

The chair he sat upon was dense wood, old and more than likely a bit brittle from the constant exposure to heat and damp from the sea, but you would not know he knew that by the position of his jaw and eyes, which were fixed on Cyclops's face as the giant performed the binding of Holmes.

"You never were given much of a chance as a child, were you?"

Cyclops ignored Holmes and set to binding his left foot to the chair.

"You were brought up in a family of four. A mother, grandmother, and aunt with no idea how to deal with the costs of raising a child your size, so they gave you up for adoption."

Cyclops began binding Holmes' other foot. But he

Flinched when Holmes had spoken and pulled a bit harder. Holmes suppressed a yelp of pain and continued.

"The home they sent you next did nothing to relieve the misery of your existence. Instead, you found yourself forced into expeditions to prey upon others for wealth. This did not earn you peace at home, love, or adoration. When you failed, you were often abused, beaten to urge you to do better. So, instead of finding encouragement, hope and a direction that would bring peace to your troubled heart...instead you were set further upon a path to a worse reputation than you already had. Now you were considered both a monster and a thief by any who knew or met you."

"Shut up!"

Holmes noted that the giant was finished, but did not leave. "Many claimed you were a monster, driven away by Odysseus. But they would have been wrong, wouldn't they? The myth of Odysseus was a lie created by Circe to protect her own image as a loving mother. But she wasn't, was she? Loving?"

Cyclops made a muffled sound, deep in his chest, like a child about to break into tears, but held it back. Barely.

Cyclops raised his eyes to investigate Holmes' face.

Holmes did not flinch at the scarred, brutal face that peered with interest into his own. The eyes were pure white with no iris. His nose was two slits in his skull. His brows jut outwards like nascent horns, framing his malformed nose below.

It was not a face that would draw forth a mother's love easily. Nor had it.

Cyclops's eyes were moist as he peered into Holmes's face. Holmes felt his own heart breaking. He did not relish his deductions but remained firm for the sake of the outcome.

"The locals thought to kill you in a fire. They failed. You learned the meaning of hatred then, in addition to abandonment and loneliness."

Cyclops snorted, a sound much like hot steam issuing from his slit nostrils. As he did, he threw his head back, revealing massive scar tissue beneath his chin, rising from his chest to his throat. Clearly made by intense heat...fire!

"And you looked at men who had a wife or lover and envied them and hated them. But..."

Cyclops sat down on his haunches, now eye to eye with Holmes, listening intently. Increasingly like a child fascinated by an old sailor's tale, not the hideous looking monster he had become.

Holmes winced inwardly. God help this poor soul, he begged silently. "...But even more than them, you hated those who could have saved you from a life of loneliness and condemned you to live a life in the shadows. A wanted creature. A monster. A dreaded Cyclops."

Driven by despair and loneliness, you looked to escape this world by burying yourself alive. Only even that escape did not work. Mesmer forced you from the sanctity of death you had made for yourself. Drew you back to a world you no longer wished to exist upon."

Cyclops let out a roar of extreme anguish and pounded his fist so hard into the deck of the ship, that the wood shattered, sending splinters flying into the air.

Holmes did not flinch. Even though he now felt beads of blood forming on his face from where some of the splinters had struck.

Cyclops reached into his filthy jacket and came out with a handkerchief. He turned it slowly, as if amused by it. "This cloth is cleaner than my soul."

He slowly dabbed the blood from Holmes's face, making a soft, clucking sound, like a mother hen. He put the handkerchief away. Looked down. Clenched his hands into fists. They became white and blood began to leak from where his ragged nails cut into the palms.

He searched Holmes's face for forgiveness, and seeing a lack of judgement, he hesitantly admitted his true feelings. "I meant no harm. I am the last of my kind. I sought companionship. But..."

Holmes saw now what he had thought, clear and obvious. He said what he must. "I do not blame you."

Cyclops gave Holmes a surprised look. He had not expected that. He had hoped for forgiveness, not understanding. His entire body quaked with emotions he had not allowed or been allowed to express for many a year. Before his self-burial and after with Mesmer, who never let him forget how unloved he was...and lonely.

It tore at his soul, and his heart.

"I find you to be quite intelligent and that is something no amount of gossip or torment can deny you."

Holmes paused a moment, then added. "I do not think you ever deserved that name first given you. It was a name meant to demean you from the beginning.

First by Circe, then by your foster parents. No, you deserve a real name. One that shows our humanity."

"Name?" Cyclops asked.

Holmes nodded. "Come closer."

Cyclops did. Holmes whispered the name he was giving Cyclops.

Holmes allowed the name to sink into Cyclops's mind. "I also see a tender heart that yearns…not for the dark justice you are now expected to perform…but for a loving hand and gentle words. Tell me I am wrong? Tell me!"

Cyclops rose to his full height, his eyes tearing up further. He saw the door to the cabin behind Holmes begin to open. He hurriedly wiped his hands on his pants. Tensed. Face blank of emotion once more.

The door behind Cyclops slammed open the rest of the way and Mesmer strode inside, wearing a garish outfit, which made him seem more a clown than a man of great magic. Which he was. "Good! You may go now; I shall have a few words with our friend."

"You will kill him?"

Mesmer eyed Cyclops, as if stunned by the question. But quickly regained his composure. His eyes narrowed. "Of course, he is going to die. What do you care? You have already murdered two of those who denied and tortured you! Why shouldn't I have the same pleasure?"

Holmes did not respond outwardly, but now another piece of the puzzle fell into place. "You made him kill them, didn't you, Mesmer? But he did not want to. You forced him. Played upon his loneliness, his abandonment and despair."

Cyclops looked at Mesmer to deny it. He did not.

Holmes continued. "You used Cyclops. Just like those you had him murder in cold blood. You are the true killer her, Mesmer, not this poor soul. You!"

Mesmer thrust an arm out and a snake of black energy struck Holmes's right arm and bit him.

Holmes howled from the pain.

"You are smart, Holmes. I'll give you that. But now I will torture you further."

"Why? Because it is the truth?"

Mesmer stepped so close to Holmes that his foul breath caused Holmes to recoil from him. "No, because I can!" He spit into Holmes's face.

Mesmer struck Holmes hard in his face, sending a spray of blood from his nose.

Cyclops raised a hand for Mesmer to stop. "No. He good man!"

"He hurt me. Badly!" Mesmer shot back, his face darkening with anger. "Just like I will now hurt him."

Cyclops made a sound of protest. "You forced me!"

Mesmer glared at Cyclops. "No wonder Odysseus was able to blind you and your brethren so easily!"

Cyclops gave Mesmer a look that made the man uneasy, but he did not give into it, he was the master and Cyclops his slave. And his magic was stronger than any mere giant. "Leave," Mesmer hissed, both hands extended, black magic swirling about them. "Now! Before I change my mind and erase the last of the Cyclops as well!"

Cyclops swiveled his face to look at Holmes. His eyes, though unseeing, seemed sad. Lost. Hurt. Like a child whose father has turned him out of his home forever.

Holmes knew that look well. He had once felt the same when he lost his original Watson. "Go. I will be fine."

Cyclops left the room, leaving the door open, but only a fraction.

Mesmer eyed Holmes sternly, his thin lips slit like the edge of a knife. "Trying to break the hold I have on that miserable creature is useless. My magic is too powerful."

"Your magic is but one of many, dear Mesmer, and it is a dark one that brings no happiness to its owner in the end."

"Do not fill my ears with all that prattle. You are a detective with no future."

"That remains to be seen!"

The hint of smoke seeps through the crack of the door.

Holmes tenses but says nothing.

"Now, we shall see if your intellect and mouth can save you now!"

Mesmer's powers gather in his eyes and his hands as he prepares to strike Holmes a terrible blow.

Main Deck

"Fire in the hold!" Screams a sailor rushing from below deck, followed soon thereafter by a score more, all fleeing to the boarding ramp to escape the roaring flames which now leap from the throat of the deck below to the main deck.

Explosions begin shaking the ship from one end to the other.

Sailors scream in terror, many diving into the Thames when the boarding ramp is shattered by an explosion there.

The First Mate, a tall fellow with a hook for his right fist turns about, unsure what to do. "Where's Master Mesmer?"

Cyclops stands there looking at him, as if dumb.

"We must save him!"

Cyclops smiles. Holds a barrel of gunpowder up in one hand and a fist clutching a torch in the other.

The First Mate screams in terror and runs for his life as Cyclops puts the torch to the barrel of gunpowder.

"Friend!" He utters, a look of peace on his face as the barrel catches fire.

The Hold

"You gain nothing by this," Holmes warns Mesmer, as he raised his hands to strike at Holmes with his magic.

Holmes smiled. "Nothing at all!"

A huge slamming sound and the door flies open to reveal the first mate laying on the corridor floor outside, flames and smoke eating at the hold.

Mesmer's face pales. "No!"

He rushes to get out.

"What about me?" Holmes casts after the fleeing man.

"You can die along with everyone else for all I care!" Mesmer cries out, his face clouded with anger.

He turns about to run and finds himself looking into the chest of Cyclops.

Two massive hands clasp Mesmer by his shoulders and lift him back inside as Cyclops enters.

"Let me go, you'll kill us both!" Mesmer shouts.

Cyclops looks at Holmes.

Holmes relaxes his chest, and the ropes fall away from his upper body and arms. He swiftly reaches down and unbinds his legs, then rises.

"I will help you," Holmes tells Cyclops.

Cyclops shakes his head.

Holmes raises a hand gently. "I swear it. Upon my very soul. I would never harm you!"

"Liar! You would kill him in an instant if able!" Mesmer shouts.

Holmes turns to him. "You are looking into a mirror of your own reflection, Mesmer. And your words that you speak as mine, are but the dark prayers of your own cruel heart!"

Cyclops shakes Mesmer and growls angrily.

Mesmer screams, "Let me go, you idiot!"

Cyclops walks all the way inside. Sets Mesmer down.

Mesmer protests. "Let me go!" He cries out in vain as Holmes stops beside Cyclops. "You do not have to do this. Let me help you!"

"Mnooo!" Cyclops wails. And for the first time probably in many, many years, Cyclops begins to cry, his sobs tearing at Holmes' heart.

Holmes puts a hand on Cyclops's arm.

"I will remember you, my friend. Always."

He rushes out the door.

Cyclops lets go of Mesmer but continues to block the door.

"Defy me, will you!"

Mesmer raises his fists to blast Cyclops with his magic. "I brought you back to life. I can send you back to death as well!"

Mesmer's fists unleash a hellfire of energies which ignite Cyclops's body with flames so fierce and hungry that he appears like a candle for a moment.

But in that moment, Mesmer sees what Cyclops has done, when the giant pulls aside his jacket to reveal sticks of dynamite wrapped about his upper body.

Cyclops smiles and says, "No friend."

The Dock

Holmes rushes between sails falling to the deck, their white canvas turning sooty black with flames, the wooden railings turning into hot burning coals. The heat is so intolerable he almost faints.

He turns about.

Decides.

Leaps.

His long, slender body arcs into the air and over the burning railing for the waters of the Thames alongside the burning vessel. He strikes the water in a steep dive, the same time as the vessel explodes, its spine breaking apart and sending the fore and aft sections of the merchant ship to the bottom of the Thames and the middle to sink slowly thereafter.

The sound of police sirens breaks up the crowd watching the horrible event.

Help Arrives Too Late

Inspector Bloodstone, Conan, Challenger, Watson, and Constable Evans jump out.

They look on in horror as the remains of the Black Goddess let out another enormous blast.

"Is this the one?" Challenger demands of Watson.

Watson is uncertain at first, then the flag of the vessel bobs into view, showing the ship's name: Black Goddess. "It is!"

The middle section of the ship blows skywards, sending them all to the planks of the platform they stand upon. A harsh rain of burning splinters, pieces of wood, metal and various mercantile products spatter them.

Finally, it stops.

Watson is the first to his feet. "Holmes!" He cries out, eyes wide with terror.

Challenger is up next, then Constable Evans and Conan, who helps the Inspector to his feet.

They all walk to the edge of the wharf to look at the burning guts and ribs of wood and steel that yet remain of the vessel as it slowly boils down into the sea water, spewing steam, further rocked by explosions of gunpowder in the bowels of its holds.

Inspector Bloodstone gives Watson a look of intense sadness. "I'm sorry, Watson."

Watson says nothing.

Challenger and Conan surround him on both sides and put a comforting hand on his arms.

Constable Evans begins to chuckle.

"You are daft, son?"

"No, father, not one bit," he replies and points.

Holmes is in the water below, clinging to a flour barrel, waving.

"Damn!" Challenger roars. Grins. "That man is like a cat with nine lives."

Conan smiles. "Oh, I'd say he has far more than that!"

Watson grabs a rope from a pile next to the edge of the pier into the water.

Holmes lets go the flour barrel and strokes for the rope.

Watson does not turn to look at the others. They would see the tears in his eyes.

Tears of joy. Of relief.

But Holmes sees them as he reaches upwards to

Watson for help to the decking. Both men have tears in their eyes. Both have loved and lost their original partners, and moments like this are powerful to them. Bringing up the memories of their loss and of their joy in finding one another again...even if different from before.

Holmes climbs onto the wharf and smiles into Watson's face. "Hug?"

Watson looks at Holmes's wet body and clothing. "Not on your life!"

They both break into laughter.

The clink of glasses, the sound of laughter, Ms. Hudson's cheerful giggles. Watson's cough of embarrassment as she kisses Holmes on his cheek.

"Well, I'm not mad, and I can say I'm glad to have you back safe and sound, Sherlock."

Holmes smiles and pats her arm. "Never any doubt of it."

Watson frowns. "I find it hard to believe that a dead man helped you, Holmes."

Holmes dabbed at his lips and shoved his dinner plate away. He took out his pipe, tamped tobacco into it, then lit it. Took a puff and pointed his pipe at Watson. "Mesmer made one huge mistake."

"You don't think he's still alive, do you?" Challenger asked, shoving a chair next to Holmes to see his face better. They had chosen to have just candlelight to make the dinner more relaxed.

Harry Houdini came up the stairs with a huge tray of steaming scones and set them on their dining table.

"I could kiss you, Harry," Watson teased.

"Better not, you'll get make up on your face," Harry warned.

Everyone laughed.

"But seriously, Holmes, how did you manage to escape that madman?" Challenger asked again.

"I wouldn't have by myself. I had help from a very good soul."

Challenger scowled. "But you said you were alone with Mesmer and Cyclops. So, who…"?

Challenger's eyes narrowed. "No. Not him. He killed two innocent souls."

Holmes frowned at him. "Challenger, who are we to judge another so harshly. They were no less guilty of murder than he."

"Why so?" Ms. Hudson asked, stunned at the rebuke.

"I researched Cyclops's life thoroughly. While investigating the two cases I found the man to have been an abandoned child, horribly abused by his parents, and his keepers at the orphanage he grew up within."

"But I thought he was a demi-God," Conan protested.

"He was. But even demi-gods can have a terrible mother. And he did."

Watson's eyebrows rose. "Circe!"

Holmes nodded. "Indeed."

"Many have such happen, and don't murder people," Conan protested.

"Yes, but the two that Cyclops murdered were two who had tortured him as a child, mutilated his body and ruined his life."

A sudden silence as everyone sat there, stunned by the revelation.

"The kindest thing I could do for him was to give him a name again. Help him to feel human. True, it does not wipe away the stain of the deaths upon his soul, but it helped give him hope."

"Of what?" Challenger asked.

"That someone cared for him. That he was not the monster everyone thought."

"But he's not a monster," Harry pointed out. The Cyclops were giants, but never monsters. Only when Circe stepped into the picture did their souls get twisted."

Watson smiled. "I rather think calling him Gifford is rather clever of you, Holmes. No one could ever call a Gifford a monster."

Challenger roared, "But he's not human and he is a monster!"

Holmes turned to Challenger. "By whose definition? Ours, or God's?"

Challenger looked away. Chastised.

Harry spoke up, "But, getting back to what you've revealed, how did you learn that Holmes?" Harry asked. "Even with my magic, I could not have read that information from their dead bodies."

"You see, Harry, it is not always what is spoken with words that evokes the truth. Sometimes it is what is not spoken."

"Well, enough of this small talk," Harry said with a snicker. "How about some magic. Real magic?"

Everyone cheered, except for Holmes, who got up. "Excuse me, I need to retire. It has been quite a trying day."

He left.

Harry took a handful of scones and began juggling them in such a way that he could take a bite of each as they rotated in his hands.

Soon they were gone.

"I can do a better trick than that, Harry!" Watson declared.

Harry frowned. Turned to Watson. "Let's see you do that trick, Watson."

"Easy." Watson said with a smirk. He grabbed a handful of scones and shoved them into his mouth at the same time.

Ms. Hudson burst into laughter.

Holmes' Room

Holmes stood at his window, looking out, the fresh night air caressing his cheeks.

"God bless your soul, Gifford. I shall never forget you. Never!"

A tear wet his eyes.

A flurry of white caused him to step back as a beautiful white dove landed on his windowsill.

It perched there, tucked its wings under and looked up at him and then he could have sworn...it smiled. Then it shot back into the air and was gone.

Holmes touched a hand over his heart.

The words of the Monk echoed in his memory that moment. "Never forget the true magic. Never! If you do, then you shall never lose your way."

Holmes smiled at the distant dove that soared upwards. "God be with you, Gifford!"

A streak of pure white light shot over the rooftops and then arrowed for the stars above.

Gifford was going home.